Herobrine In Real Life

ALSO BY AJ DIAZ

THE TAYLOR KELSEY MYSTERY SERIES
Mystery of the 19th Hole
Mystery of the 101st Meter
Mystery of the 33rd Chess Piece
Mystery of the 51st Star
Mystery of the 13th Floor
Mystery of the 25th Hour
Mystery of the Second Name

MINECRAFT NOVELS w/ Jake Turner
Herobrine In Real Life
Minecraft High School
Fright Night

STEAMPUNK SERIES
Catherine
Tiffany (Coming 2019)

Follow AJ Diaz on Social Media.
Instagram: @theAJDiaz

Herobrine In Real Life
An Unofficial Minecraft Adventure

by

AJ Diaz

// with Jake Turner //

MORE BY JAKE TURNER

For updates, a newsletter, and cool free stuff visit:
itlpress.com/minecraft

MORE BY JAKE TURNER

For updates, a newsletter, and cool free stuff visit:
itlpress.com/minecraft

Episode 1

1

Herobrine.

HEROBRINE.

HEROBRINE!!!!!!!!!!!!!!!

He is the scariest person in all of Minecraft. I agree with Henry about this. I mean, Henry is scared of everything, but I AM actually scared of Herobrine.

This story I'm about to tell you is actually pretty scary.

If you're a little kid who can barely handle scary stories, then you should put this book down, and maybe even burn it (that's probably a bad idea. I almost burned my house down the other day. My parents were NOT happy!).

Well, don't burn it.

But hide it.

Because this book is all about Herobrine, and about how Herobrine came into our world, the REAL WORLD. Herobrine came to planet Earth.

You may have read my last book. It's about how Minecraft came into real life. That was the first time Minecraft, and characters from the game like Steve and the Wither Boss, came into our world. The bad thing was that Herobrine realized he could also come into our world. And since apparently he had nothing to do back in the world of Minecraft, he decided to come try to destroy our world.

My name is Stevi, BTW, and I'm a girl with a sort of boy name.

But I really like my name.

I'm ten years old now. When Minecraft came into the world the first time, I was only nine and I was just a little kid. I know a lot more things now, and this is a crazy story.

It's a true story.

So listen up.

A little more about me: I play Minecraft anywhere from two hours a day—sometimes less if I'm grounded—to five or ten hours a DAY. Basically, Minecraft is my life. I watch DanTDM every morning. I've been watching him since before he had blue hair. I love Jemma and his cute little pugsies. I asked my mom for pugs and she told me, "no and pugs are ugly."

Well, pooh.

I think pugs are cute.

But here's the point, people!

Herobrine came into the real freakin' world!

It all started on the night I decided to sneak out of my house after my parents were asleep. Don't worry. I had good reasons. I was trying to catch a fish.

2

I'm not particularly a *fish* type of person. Nope, I wouldn't say that I am. I've only ever been fishing one time with one of my uncles, and he never let me catch the fish. He said I was too small. Pooh on him, because he kept getting his fishing line stuck on rocks and various underwater things.

Anyway, no one taught me how.

But tonight, I would FISH!

The whole thing started earlier today, after school. I was walking home with some friends and some frenemies, and we were walking by some old abandoned property. I said we should explore it because we had some time. Some of the girls didn't want to because they didn't want to get dirty. But some of the guys wanted to.

The abandoned lot is quite large and filled with all kinds of different trees and big bushes and little ponds. We began climbing the trees and finding cool places to make forts in the bushes.

And then, hidden behind a hedge of big bushes, was something we'd never seen before: a large pond. We were amazed to find one back here. I had no idea there was one back here. If I'd known, I'd have been back here ALL THE TIME—when I wasn't playing Minecraft, of course. Immediately we found a bunch of crawdads in the pond and started catching them. And then we noticed there were fish.

None of us could explain how the fish got in the pond back here. Maybe there used to be a lake, or maybe someone just put the fish in the pond. Either way, we tried catching the fish, but we didn't have fishing poles. I said I would be the first one to catch one of the fish.

All the guys said they would be the first.

But then some old people found us and told us to get off the property. I told my friends we needed to sneak out and catch one of the fish tonight. It was our last chance.

I don't know why it was our "last" chance, but I felt like it was.

So I waited until it got dark outside, until after dinner.

Then I waited for my parents to go to bed. I was supposed to go to bed at ten o'clock myself. When it became ten thirty, I got out of my bed and walked quietly down the hall to my parents' room. Their TV wasn't on anymore. I peeked my head in the door and saw them both laying there. My dad was already snoring.

It was time.

Now, just so you know, I don't normally sneak out. This would technically only be my fourth time. Well, now that I think about it, I guess I do sneak out a lot.

It's very dangerous.

But at least I wouldn't be alone out there. Some of the guys said they'd sneak out as well. Besides, it wasn't as scary to me as fighting Herobrine in Minecraft.

Which reminded me.

Where was Henry?

I needed him.

Henry was my next-door neighbor and my best friend. He was in the other book I wrote about the first time Minecraft came into real life. He was sometimes a scaredy-cat, but he was always there when you needed him. He also loved Minecraft just as much as I. One difference from me is that he never got in trouble. He was a really good kid. I admired him for it, but sometimes it bugged me because he didn't like to sneak out at night with me to go on adventures!

I was also jealous that he was home schooled. He got to wear his pajamas all day and got to play Minecraft during his lunch break for, like, TWENTY minutes.

Anyway, I needed his help tonight if my plan was going to work. For one, he said he had a fishing pole, and I needed one. Two, I needed him to lay in my bed and cover for me just in case my parents came to check on me. He could just put the covers over his head so they couldn't see him.

This way, I knew for sure I wouldn't get caught.

I was already out of bed. I closed my bedroom door just in case Henry made a lot of noise climbing through the window. Then I opened my window. A screen was still in it, but I pushed it out and it fell down to the floor outside the house.

My room was on the second story, so Henry would have to climb up. It was okay, though, because there was a drainage pipe on the side of the house he could climb. I'd climbed up it a cajillion times. Henry wasn't that good of a climber, but I believed in him. Maybe.

Anyway, I looked around and didn't see him anywhere. He was supposed to be here by now. I sat in the window, watching, waiting.

Finally, I called Henry on the phone. Henry and I both had cell phones. He answered after a few rings.

"Hello."

"Henry! Where are you?" I snapped.

"I don't know if I can come over."

"What? Why?"

"What if I get in trouble?"

"Henry," I said, "you never do anything wrong. Your parents would never think to check your room. My parents already caught me sneaking out one time, which is why I need your help."

"But what if my mom finds out?"

"Then you'll probably only get in trouble for a week, because they'll go easy on you, because you never get in trouble. I always get in trouble. If they catch me again, I'll get in trouble for a whole month probably. Maybe even a year. Then we couldn't play Minecraft for a year. Would you want that?"

"Well... No."

"So get your butt over here."

"But, Stevi—"

"Henry, I don't have time for all of this. If I don't catch that fish first, then we're going to lose."

"I'm afraid of getting in trouble."

"Henry, you'll only get in trouble for a day or a week. Maybe two weeks at the worst, but that's not as bad as a month. I need your help."

"Fine," he finally said.

"Follow the plan," I said, and I hung up.

I was getting impatient. I needed to get out to that pond ASAP. My entire reputation depended on it. I pictured myself catching one of those giant fishes first. Imagine it!

I paced about while I waited for Henry.

3

The Tale of Herobrine

There was once a Minecraft character named Steve and a character named Hero. And also Alex. The three of them were best friends.

When they were young, they all went to the same school. They hung out everyday for hours a day—they fished together, mined together, fought zombies together. They were a team.

Until that horrible day.

Nobody knows exactly how it happened, but there was a glitch in Minecraft's code. Hero was a very nice and friendly person, but his name got changed to Hero-brine, and he became an evil person. He immediately tried to kill Steve and Alex, and Steve and Alex had to run away.

Herobrine, as he was now called, didn't know what had happened to himself. He became sad that he'd tried to kill his friends, and he ran away and secluded himself in a mountain, where he built his home.

Every once in a while, he couldn't control his rage—he

would leave the mountain, destroy a city, and then go back to his house in the mountain.

Herobrine was super powerful, and nobody could defeat him. Steve and Alex were so sad that Hero had turned evil. They decided one day to go to Herobrine's mountain and try to talk to him, hoping they could all be friends once more. But Herobrine attacked them and tried to kill them. They got away, barely escaping with their lives.

They knew that there was no hope for Herobrine.

They stayed far away from him.

And they never saw him again.

4

If I got caught, my parents would probably hate me. I already knew they didn't like me, because I got in trouble ALL THE TIME. This is why it was crucial that Henry help me.

I sat in my open window, waiting, waiting, waiting…

Henry finally showed up. I saw him in the side yard of his house, climbing his fence into my backyard. It took him a couple tries to get onto his fence, and he was making a lot of noise.

Stupid Henry.

He was making me angry.

He was going to wake up a grown up. Grown ups wake up surprisingly easily.

Then he jumped down into my backyard and went to the bottom of the window. I shook the drain pipe to signal to him that he should began climbing it. He stared up at me, then at the pipe in front of him, then up at me. I could tell he was scared.

"Don't be scared," I half-whispered and half-shouted down to him.

"I am, though," he said back.

"Shhhh!"

"I don't know if I can do this, Stevi."

"You can!"

It took him a long minute, which was making me impatient, to finally begin the climb. It wasn't that hard. I'd done it a lot.

Finally, he got up to my window. I grabbed him by the shirt to make sure he didn't fall, and I yanked him into the room. He fell onto the floor and groaned.

"Ouch. Jeez, Stevi."

"Calm down, Henry."

He was rubbing his arm, which had gotten rubbed against the carpet. Then he got to his feet, looking very angry with me.

His sheep-head was looking particularly sheep-y tonight. For those who don't already know, Henry has a crazy mop of hair on top of his head. Not a literal mop. It's just a thing adults say. It means that he has really messy and floppy hair. It's always everywhere.

Poor kid.

I would have buzzcut his head already, but he gets mad when I mention it.

He looks like a sad sheep, most of the time.

Right now, he looked like a sad and angry sheep.

I didn't know what to say to him, so I just said, "Stop being such a noob."

"I'm not a noob."

"It took you a long time to climb that."

"Well, I didn't want to."

Henry was bugging me. But I needed to go catch that fish. I realized he'd forgotten the fishing pole. I snapped at him, "Where's the fishing pole?"

His face went white. "I forgot it."

"Henry. Stupid!"

I tried to keep my voice down.

His eyes sunk, his head sunk. He sat on the floor. Ashamed.

I didn't have time for this.

"I'm going to leave now. I'll catch the fish some other way. I'll just have to jump in the pond." I grabbed my high-powered flashlight from off my dresser and clipped it to my belt. The flashlight worked under the freakin' water! Which is why I'd asked for it for Christmas.

I climbed out of my window and held onto the drainpipe. Henry was still sitting there with all his hair flopped to one side, looking sad.

"Thanks, Henry," I said, feeling a little bad for him.

He didn't move or respond for a few big seconds. Then he finally said, "I want to go to the pond with you."

"I want you to come," I said. "But I need you to cover for me here."

He nodded.

I climbed down the pipe. Then I began running down the street, for the secret pond!

5

Sure, I felt a little bad for how I'd treated Henry. But he was such a noob. He'd forgotten the only thing he was supposed to remember. It was like when we play Minecraft and he forgets the basic things when we go mining—like steaks and/or a bucket of water.

He was a noob a lot of the time.

I made fun of him a lot for it, but he deserved it.

He'd forgotten the fishing pole. The whole point of this night was for me to catch this fish.

It didn't matter, I told myself. I was sure I would catch this fish anyway.

The street was sort of dark, but there were a lot of tall streetlights. They were all white. The property was a few blocks away, and I didn't stop running until I got there. A few cars passed me on the way, but they didn't stop or anything. I didn't run into any adults out here, so that was good. I was afraid I'd run into one who knew me and they would tell my parents on me. Or would tell me to go home. Or, the worst scenario, an adult would try to kidnap me. But I already had a plan if that happened. I would jump over a fence into someone's backyard. I never saw adults jump fences (only policemen). They probably wouldn't follow me. I'd be okay. I'm tough, and I climb fences really fast. I practice all the time.

I didn't use my flashlight until I got to the abandoned property.

My frenemies were supposed to be here, but I didn't see them yet. I hoped they weren't going to wimp out on me. If I was going to catch this fish, I needed them to see it, and I couldn't really bring the fish to school in my backpack. And if I took a picture of the fish on my phone, they would probably say I photoshopped it. Which is dumb, because I don't know any ten-year-old who knows how to work photoshop, but that's always what they tell me when I do something cool and take a picture of it. Like, one time I was walking down the street and I saw a random colorful bird, and I got close enough to get a selfie with it. They all told me I used photoshop. *I don't even have photoshop!* I just play Minecraft.

Once I made it to the property, I took out my flashlight. It was a tiny bit scary out here in the darkness, but I decided not to think about it. I began walking over the dirt, past the bushes, and under the trees, deeper into the dark and lonely property. I swept my flashlight beam all around, looking for my friends. I didn't see them. They must not have gotten here yet.

That's when someone dropped down from one of the trees and screamed!

I punched the person immediately in the face and he fell to the floor.

"Stevi! Wait, stop, it's just me," the boy screamed. And I realized it was just Edwin.

A few other boys climbed down from the tree.

One of them said, "We were going to try to scare you."

I crossed my arms. "Are you ready to fish or not?"

They were all here. Four of them. Edwin, Zachary, Zachary 2, and Zachary 3. I couldn't wait to catch that fish. Two of them had flashlights, but mine was more powerful than theirs.

We got to the pond, which involved climbing and fighting through the thick bushes, and before they could stop me or say anything, I jumped into the FREEZING cold waters.

6

I wished Henry could see me now.

I mean, even though he was a noob and had a sheep head, he was still my best friend. He was better than all these boys, who were all dumb. Zachary 3 was the worst. And he farted all the time. He thought it was the funniest thing ever, but it was really just gross. I punched him a lot. I had no choice. Henry was much better than all of these guys.

Back to the water!

It was freezing cold. I was wearing clothes, not a bathing suit, and they made me feel heavy in the water. My teeth starting chattering immediately, but I only needed to be in the pond for long enough to catch a fish.

My feet were on the ground and the water was up to my shoulders. I walked further into the pond. All the guys were yelling that my jump was awesome. They were shining their flashlights around like crazy, which was kind of annoying.

I turned back to them. "Jump in, scaredy cats."

Zachary 3 didn't hesitate. He jumped in with a big

splash and popped his head out, waving his long hair every which way like a dog. The water flew off onto me.

"Gross hair water," I said.

"My hair's not gross."

"You're gross."

"Yes," he said with a smile.

I looked at the other three guys.

"We have to hold the flashlights," one said.

"Fine," I said.

My flashlight was already submerged under the water, which was awesome. The beam of light illuminated the pond's floor, which was really muddy. When I took steps, it caused mud to rise up and cause the clear water to become murky. Other than that, the water was pretty clear.

"You didn't bring a fishing pole, Stevi," said Edwin.

"No duh," I said, aiming my flashlight around, looking for the fish. "Do you see it, Zack?" I asked. He didn't answer. I looked over and he was splashing around.

"Stop," I said.

"Why?"

"You're going to wake up the fish."

"What?"

"Yeah, they're probably sleeping. It'll make them easier to catch."

"Fish don't sleep."

"Of course they do."

"No, they don't," shouted Edwin from the side of the pond.

"You don't know anything," I said.

"Hahaha, Stevi thinks fish sleep."

Ugh, these boys were the dumbest.

Finally, after a whole long minute, my flashlight beam found a fish. It was a pretty big fish, about a foot long and pretty meaty. It would make good food. I wasn't going to eat it, though, because my parents would probably be mad if I brought home a big fish. They would wonder where I'd gotten it from and ask all kinds of questions. I could invent a story—like some random guy gave me the fish. But I didn't think they'd believe it. Plus, it's not good to lie.

I began creeping toward the fish like the fish snatcher that I was. One slow step at a time. I had to shush Zachary 3 a few times because he was splashing and singing behind me. I took another step, and another. The fish was floating halfway between the floor and the surface of the water. The water was up to my neck now. I was pretty sure the fish was asleep.

I knew I had to be fast once I got close.

Another careful step…

"One small step for Stevi," I whispered to myself. "One giant step for fish-kind."

That's when, from behind us, we heard a giant and LOUD gunshot! We all spun around and saw a man coming through the bushes. "Kids! What are you doing?!" he yelled.

And he shot the gun again.

7

This was basically a terrible situation.

A man with a gun, probably the man who owned this property, was climbing through the bushes, towards us! Did I mention he had a *gun?!*

None of us were dead yet, so he must have been firing the gun into the air to scare us or he just had really bad aim. Either way, I was really scared. I had never imagined this could happen.

I wondered if this was how Henry felt when he is afraid. I'm hardly ever afraid, so I wasn't use to this. Zachary 3 and I ran, splashing like crazy, to the other end of the pool of water. I didn't know what the other Zacharies and Edwin were doing.

I clambered and clawed for the opposite edge of the pond and threw myself towards it. I scraped my hands alongside the muddy dirt embankment and got to my feet, Zachary 3 just behind me. On our feet, we burst into the nearest giant bushes, running away from the angry man with the gun. The branches and thorns scratched us all from all directions because we didn't have time to be careful. Branches were scratching against my ears and forehead. I pushed ahead, trying to keep some of them away from my face with my hands. My flashlight was still on. I figured I should probably turn it off so the guy couldn't see where we were.

I hoped all my other frenemies were okay.

I was really glad Henry hadn't come. I didn't like it when he was in danger. He was sort of helpless most of the time, and I always felt like it was my responsibility to protect him.

Another gunshot split the air around us!

I looked at Zack. He hadn't been shot. I was still good.

"He's just trying to scare us," I said.

"It's working," Zack said, and he let out a big fart.

"Stupidhead," I said as we continued through the tangly brush.

We finally made it out the other side of the bushes. There wasn't much to see back here. Only more abandoned property. It was basically a big field with overgrown weeds. We could barely see, though, because there were no streetlights and the moon wasn't very big tonight.

I shined on my flashlight.

And standing right there was a man in an ALL WHITE SUIT. He was holding a big gun—looked like what I'm pretty sure shotguns look like. He was wearing a white top-hat.

"Well, well," he said. "What do we have here?"

I was stunned. I didn't know what to say or do. I couldn't run back into the bushes because the man with the other gun was coming from that way.

"You'll never kill us," I said finally.

I heard movement off to the sides of the man. I shined my light to his right and saw a woman in a white fancy suit standing there with a pistol in her hand. She began walking towards me. I shined my light to the left and saw another man in a white suit.

"Who are you people?" I asked.

But before I could do anything, and before they answered, the woman on the right lifted up her pistol and shot me. A little dart shot right into my belly button! It stung. And that was the last thing that I remembered.

8

Steve had never told Alex the full story of Herobrine. He didn't know how to tell her the truth. See, in Minecraft, as in all video games, there were glitches.

The truth about their old friend Hero was that he hadn't been glitch-ed for no reason. Steve remembered the day it happened. Alex hadn't been there. She didn't know.

Steve was in Minecraft right now, at the top of his tall house, overlooking the valley. The block sun was going down, and he was thinking about that day, a long time ago, when Hero had become Hero*brine*.

Steve and Hero were walking home from school. Alex was out sick. She'd stayed home that day. And they were surrounded by the school bullies. The bullies, for some reason, didn't pick on Steve. They only picked on Hero. They started to fight him, started beating him up. Steve didn't do anything about it. He didn't try to save Hero. He simply ran away. Because he was scared.

That was the day that the glitch happened and Hero turned into Herobrine. Sometimes Steve wondered if there had never been a glitch. And he wondered if maybe Hero had decided to turn evil all on his own. But that was a crazy thought. Why would Hero just decide to turn evil? It must have been a glitch in the code. It was the only thing that made sense.

That was a long time ago.

Herobrine had caused a lot of destruction since then and had destroyed a lot of towns. But now he'd gone to planet Earth. His mission was to destroy Earth. Steve knew this, but Alex didn't know it yet. Herobrine had just escaped the game into Earth two days ago.

When Alex found out, she would want to go to Earth to try and save it.

But Steve knew the truth: Herobrine was too powerful. They wouldn't be able to stop him from destroying Earth even if they tried.

Which is why Steve decided not to try. He decided he would just stay within the Minecraft game, stay home, stay safe. Earth would be destroyed, and there was nothing he could do about it.

9

Henry was bored.

And also really scared.

Stevi's door was closed and he sat beside it, listening for her parents. If he heard them walking around beyond the door, he would jump into the bed and cover himself up under the covers. And he would try not to make any noises. He would have to act like he was sound asleep so they wouldn't ask questions. So far, though, nothing had happened.

Everything was okay.

He wondered what his parents would do if they found out he'd snuck out and left his bedroom after ten thirty at night! This was the first time he'd done anything this bad.

Part of him did want to be at the pond with Stevi. Even though he hated adventure, he sometimes liked it. He felt safe with Stevi because she always knew what to do. No matter what bad things happened or what bad situations they found themselves in, she always saved them and always knew what to do. Henry liked that, because he never knew what to do and was afraid almost all the time.

10

I had no earthly idea what I was supposed to do. I didn't even know where I was. I'd woken up and my eyes were closed. I was afraid to open them. I was afraid to find out where I was. I'd been kidnapped by people in white suits. Why? Why would they even want me?

I could hear them talking. Which is why I didn't want to open my eyes. I decided to pretend I was asleep, listen to them, and hopefully find out who they were.

One of them was saying, "Blah. Blah, blah, blah. Blah."

The other one answered, "Blahhhhh!"

One of them made noises as if he were a sheep.

None of this made sense.

I snapped my eyes open. They all looked at me. And I saw where we were. I nearly screamed and I couldn't breathe for a few moments.

We were in a Minecraft flying machine. We were flying over my neighborhood, and we were high up in the sky! The pistons weren't making any noise because they'd been gelled with slime balls. We were flying pretty fast. All the homes beneath us looked small.

And that was another crazy thing—the entire inside of this plane was made of glass blocks, so I could see directly beneath us. I could see all the streetlights and stoplights and local baseball and football stadium lights. It looked really pretty.

I started breathing again and looked at the white-suited people. There were four of them and they were all looking at me like I was an alien. One of them was a woman, and three of them were big strong-looking men.

"What do you guys want?"

"We want you," said the woman. "You're Stevi, right?"

"Yes," I said.

And then I recognized her. She was one of the Minecraft game makers, one of the programmers. She'd visited my school when I fought the wither boss in my last book. I didn't remember her name.

"I'm Larissa," she said. "We're glad you're here."

"Where are you taking me?"

I was really confused.

"We need your help."

The woman switched spots with one of the men so she could sit next to me. "Honey, sweetie pie, small person," she said, which was a weird string of words to call me, "we're very glad you're here, because something very bad has happened, and we need your help."

She tried to hold my hand to make me feel better but I swatted it away.

She took back her hand, gasping. "How rude?" she said. And then she stuck her hand in her mouth to suck on it as if it were a piece of meat. It was really weird.

"Why are you all so weird?"

One of the men moaned like a sheep, opening his mouth really wide. "Ba-a-a-a-a-a-a-a."

One of the men seemed to have an itch on his face. But instead of simply itching it, he started throwing up his hand toward his face and slapping himself.

"What's wrong with him?"

Larissa turned my jaw towards her. "Stevi, sweetie, princess of Minecraft, I have some very important news to tell you."

"Well, don't call me all those things."

I was confused, and scared, and getting angry now. I put a scowl on my face. Larissa didn't seem to care. She told me the news: "Minecraft has come into real life again."

Even though I was angry, I smiled. I was going to get to see Steve again. He is a good friend of mine. "Where is Steve?"

"Steve hasn't come into our world. Herobrine has come into our world."

I was speechless. I didn't know what to say.

If Herobrine was in our world…

I got chills, because I was so suddenly scared.

The sheep guy made another sheep noise.

We continued flying through the air, everything quiet except the sheep man. He made a few more noises but then Larissa told him to keep his mouth shut.

"What does this mean?" I finally asked.

I was really afraid of Herobrine.

"His plan," said Larissa. "Is to destroy the entire world. Which is why we need your help."

11

It was cool being in this flying machine. These white suit people were still scary to me, though, because they'd chased us all down and they'd shot me with a sleeping dart. In my belly button. I checked my belly button to see if the dart was still there. It wasn't.

"If you needed my help, why didn't you just ask me?" I said. "Why did you kidnap me?"

"We didn't know how to approach," said Larissa.

"You shot me!" I said.

"Only with a sleeping dart."

"How'd you like to be shot with a sleeping dart?"

"I'm sorry, love cakes, love pie, sugar dear."

I blinked. This lady was insane in the membrane. Like, seriously lady. I decided to call her weird names back. "Apology not accepted, crazy lady, cat lady, weirdo."

The sheep noise guy looked at me as if I'd said a bad word. He looked right into my eyes, then he opened his mouth really wide and said, "Ba—a—a—a-a—a-a."

"You're dumb," I said. "Stop."

Larissa laughed at the whole thing like it was funny.

"Well, next time, just ask me," I said.

"Okay, sweet—"

"And why are you all wearing white suits?"

"Because white is a great color," said Larissa.

I couldn't figure these people out. But I had met Larissa before. I didn't remember her being this weird. She'd actually seemed kind of normal before. Then I realized something else.

"What did you guys do with Edwin and Zack 1, Zack 2, and Zack 3?"

One of the men finally spoke up: "We drowned them in the pond."

"What?!" I yelled in horror.

He started laughing. "Just kidding!"

"What?!" I yelled again, angry and still in horror.

"We didn't drown them."

"Why would you say that?" I said.

"You're scaring her," said Larissa.

"You're making me mad," I said, because that was mostly what was happening. "What did you really do with them?" I asked.

"We tied them to a tree," he said.

"You tied them to *what* tree?"

"We tied them to a tree on that property."

"Well, you can't just tie people up."

The man shrugged. "Why not?"

These were the dumbest and weirdest adults.

We were still flying through the air and my neighborhood was far behind us. "Where are we going?"

"We'll explain on the way," said Larissa.

"No," I said. "You'll explain now."

I looked around. I needed to get out of here. I could

break one of the glass blocks, but I couldn't jump down because I'd die from the fall. We were really high up in the air. Thousands of feet high!

"Look," said Larissa, "I'm sorry about all the commotion, but we really do need your help. What would put your mind at ease?"

I didn't want to be up here any more.

"You say Herobrine is in my world. What am I supposed to do about it?"

"You're supposed to stop him."

"I don't know how. Why me? Why don't you get the army to help you?"

"And start a war? No. We need to keep Herobrine as secret from the public eye as possible. Nobody can know he's here."

"Well, they are going to know when he starts destroying our planet!"

"He's already started," she said. "But luckily the world hasn't noticed yet because he popped into our world in South America, in the jungles. Only remote villages know about him. He's destroying villages. But the rest of South America doesn't know about him yet, and he hasn't been in the news yet. This is our chance to stop him before a lot of people get scared."

"You're just afraid that when people find out they're going to think it's your fault. That's why, huh?"

"Do you want to help save the world or not?" she asked.

I crossed my arms. I *did* want to help save the world. The problem was, I didn't know how to stop Herobrine. I was too scared to even play him in the game. But I thought about it for a minute, and I realized that I'm only scared of things in video games and movies—I'm not actually scared of anything in real life. Maybe Herobrine in real life wouldn't be as scary as he is in the game.

"We're asking you," explained Larissa, "because you're the only one who's defeated the wither boss in real life. You have Minecraft skills."

I uncrossed my arms. "Fine." But then I recrossed my arms. "But I have a few conditions."

12

Two old people were going on a late night walk with their dogs. As they walked by the old abandoned property, the old guy saw four boys tied to a tree. One of them was tied to a tree trunk. Two of them were tied to overhead branches and they were hanging upside-down. The last one was tied to one of the hanging ones, and he was also hanging.

All the boys were screaming. "Help! Help!"

The old man stopped and put a hand to his forehead, peering at them. "How did all you whippersnappers get into that tree?"

"It's a crazy story!" one of them yelled. "Can you get us down?"

"I'll have to get my knife. I'll be back."

Edwin watched the old man and woman incredibly, very, super slowly turn around and begin walking back to their house so the old man could get a knife so that he could help cut them out of this tree. They were walking so slow!

"Faster!" Edwin yelled. "Please. Faster!"

It took the old man like a minute just to take one step!

The Zacharies started yelling as well. "Faster! Old farts are so slow!"

The old people didn't even seem to hear them.

"We're going to be stuck here all night at this rate," said Edwin.

That's when a Minecraft flying machine swooped onto the property in front of them and parked. It was really dark out here so they couldn't see who was in the machine. But then they saw the white suited people get out of the flying machine and begin walking towards them.

"Go away!" shouted Zachary 1. He was very afraid. These were the people that had tied them to this tree.

One of the men made a sheep noise. Which made Zachary 2 and 3 scream and Zachary 1 cry. Edwin made a sheep noise back, mocking the guy. But the guy only made another sheep noise in return. Edwin hoped the old guy would come back right about now to save them, but he realized that would never happen. The guy was so slow it would probably take him an hour to get back.

But then Edwin saw Stevi climb out of the flying machine.

What was she doing?

"Stevi, what are you doing?" he asked.

"We need your help," she said.

13

Henry was falling asleep on the floor. Stevi's parents hadn't woken up and his parents hadn't been over here looking for him, so it seemed like the night was a success. As he began to doze off, he began dreaming of pizza and Ninja Turtles. They got to eat pizza all the time. He wished he was a Ninja Turtle and could eat pizza all the time. But you have to have a car so you can go to the pizza place. Or you have to have a credit card so you can call the pizza place and pay for your pizza. He thought about it for awhile and realized he didn't actually know the process of how to order a pizza. He'd figure it out when he grew up. He made a note-to-self to pay attention next time his parents ordered pizza. He loved pepperoni and sausage. And pineapple.

He wasn't near the window, but he heard footsteps coming from outside the window. He heard people making noises, snickers and giggles and talking. They were walking up the driveway toward the house. He heard what sounded like a grown up making a sheep noise.

"Baa-aa-a—a-a-a—a-aa."

It was kind of unsettling.

Henry got to his feet, wide awake now, confused.

He walked slowly toward the window and the noises got louder. There was definitely a group of people, and then he heard the drain pipe was making noise. Someone was climbing up! He heard another sheep-like call.

"Bahh-ah-ahh-!"

Henry didn't know what to do. He wasn't trained for this. These people could be robbers. But then Stevi's blonde head popped up past the windowsill. She pulled herself into the room and fell onto the soft carpeted floor.

Then a man's head popped up above the windowsill. He opened his mouth really wide and made a really loud sheep noise! Henry nearly screamed, but Stevi grabbed his mouth and stopped the scream. Then she pointed her finger at the sheep guy and yelled in a harsh whisper: "I told you to stop that! Get down."

The man pushed himself away from the wall and let himself fall down to the floor. They were two stories high! They heard the man land and groan in pain.

"He's really, *really* dumb," said Stevi.

"Who is he?" Henry asked, confused by this whole situation.

"He works for Minecraft. The company."

"Are they still mad at us?"

"No. They need our help."

"Our help? Why our help?"

"They need us to stop Herobrine. He got into real life and he's going to destroy the world."

Henry gulped. "You're just playing a joke on me, right?"

"No, Henry. It's real."

"Why would they ask us? We're just kids."

"Because we're the only ones who know how to fight the mobs in real life."

Henry gulped again.

"Edwin and the three Zacks are going to help us too."

"Edwin is my mortal enemy!" Henry yelled, too loudly.

Stevi shushed him, putting a finger to her mouth. Then she flung her arm behind her. "We need all the help we can get. This is Herobrine we're talking about for crying out loud!"

"When are we supposed to fight him?"

"Tonight," Stevi said.

There was a pause. Henry was trying to think.

"I should probably brush my teeth first," he finally said.

"No," said Stevi. "That's not important right now. We need to go. Herobrine is destroying villages in South America as we speak."

"Should I bring pajamas?"

"No, you noob!"

"Stop calling me that."

"Right now," said Stevi, "we only need to worry about Herobrine. He's destroying villages and hurting people and probably killing them too! So stop being a noob, okay?"

"This is happening fast."

"We have no choice," said Stevi.

That was true, thought Henry. The Minccraft people were right for recruiting Stevi. She was the best Minecraft fighter he knew. And she'd killed the wither boss in real life when it was trying to destroy their school.

If anyone could fight Herobrine, it was Stevi. But then

he remembered something. "But, Stevi, you're afraid of Herobrine."

And suddenly Henry was afraid. Normally, when he was with Stevi, he was never afraid because she was never afraid. But he knew that Stevi was afraid of Herobrine.

"I won't be," she said. "I need your help, Henry. I couldn't have saved our world against the wither boss except that you'd helped me. You saved the world too and basically helped defeat the wither boss too. You're smarter than me about Minecraft, and I'm a good fighter. You're the only one I can trust. I don't trust Edwin or these Minecraft people. I need you to have my back, and be my best friend."

"I am your best friend," he said. "I'll go. Of course I'll go."

Stevi hugged him.

14

Henry and I snuck downstairs in my house to the kitchen because we needed to fill a backpack up with essential supplies: food, snacks, chocolate, and more food.

We actually decided to fill up two backpacks.

We would each need a flashlight. My dad had an extra one in the garage. And probably our Gameboys because it was a really long flight down to South America.

And sweatshirts.

Henry's clothes were back at his house, and we didn't want to risk waking up his parents, so he had to borrow one of my sweatshirts and backpacks. My only backup sweatshirt was pink.

"The guys will make fun of me," he said.

"Oh pooh," I said. "It doesn't matter if they do. It only matters if you're warm."

"Fine," he whispered back, putting it on.

We were back in my room now, looking through the backpacks of snacks that we'd packed: we packed the candy we'd found—Snickers Bars, Twix, and Reeses Cups —some granola bars (which were really healthy, my mom always says), some water bottles (water is really important), and some dates (which are delicious and Indiana Jones likes them and he's the greatest explorer!).

With all of these things, we would be ready for this great adventure.

I wasn't sure if we'd be ready to take on Herobrine. We'd need Minecraft weapons, potions and enchantments, but I figured we'd get those when we got closer to Herobrine. There was a box in the flying machine, and I'm pretty sure it had supplies in it because it was double wide.

It was only Henry and I in my room. We had our sweatshirts on and we put the backpacks over our shoulders. Everyone else was waiting for us outside. And since it was just Henry and I, I lowered my voice really low. "Remember, Henry, I don't trust any of these people. The boys will help us fight Herobrine, but the adults are acting really weird. I don't trust them."

"I got your back, Stevi," he said.

"Good," I said.

Then I put out my hand to shake his.

We shook hands.

Then we went to the window, and climbed out.

15

The flying machine was pretty big, but there were more of us in it now than the adults had counted on. There were the four boys, plus Henry, plus me, plus Larissa, plus three grown up men. We all had our own seats but there wasn't much room to lay down. I wanted to lay down and sleep. Instead, I just leaned my head against Henry. He was already falling asleep. His head leaned back down against mine and his sheepish hair fell on me.

At least he was clean, unlike the other boys.

I made sure they were sitting on the other side of our little glass Minecraft plane. Whenever Zack 3 had to fart, we made him climb up onto the roof of the machine so that way he didn't poison the air inside of here, where we were trying to sleep.

Basically, the flying machine took off high into the sky. We were far above the neighborhoods, and after an hour we were far away from our hometown.

It was a crazy thought—just a few hours ago I hadn't ever expected Minecraft to come back into real life. Well, I'd always had hope that Minecraft would come back into real life, but my hope was that Steve would come back to visit me, not that Herobrine would enter the world.

I wondered how it had happened. It must have been the Minecraft programmers' faults since they were the ones trying to cover it up.

Only a few hours ago, I was living my life and my only main goal was catching that mega fish in that hidden pond. Now I was in a Minecraft flying machine, soaring over America. Headed towards South America. It would take us all night to get there, Larissa said. So it would be a good idea to sleep. It was past eleven o'clock at night right now, almost midnight. I usually didn't stay up this late and I was tired.

I was having a hard time falling asleep, though, because there was something strange about this whole thing. It was like I'd told Henry, I didn't trust these adults. Larissa was a cool person—WAS. Now she was just a weirdo psycho lady. Last time I saw her she was very normal. And why were they all wearing white dress-up suits? It didn't make sense. That's not how adults are supposed to dress unless they're going to a dress-up party. If they were wearing normal black or grey suits it would make sense. And why did that guy keep making sheep noises?

Right now, he was asleep, so that was nice.

I could tell by the way Henry was breathing that he was fast asleep. I would need to fall asleep as soon as possible. We had a big day ahead of us.

I only thought of my parents one time. I knew they'd be mad at me when this was all over, but I didn't have time to worry about it. They'd probably be very worried when they couldn't find me tomorrow. But Herobrine would destroy the world if I didn't do anything about it.

I had a major doubt in my gut. Usually all of my "gut feelings" told me that I could win. Right now, my gut was telling me, for the first time, that I wasn't sure if I could defeat Herobrine.

I looked at all the people here, one by one, before I closed my eyes.

The Zacks were pretty good at running and being athletic. Not as good as me, but pretty good. Edwin wasn't a nice boy. He was actually sometimes very evil. Something happened between him and Henry in the last story, but I never found out what happened between them except they both didn't like each other. Edwin was a giant meanie, but he was more athletic than me a lot of the time. That would be a good thing for us.

I didn't trust the adults.

The best person here was my best friend Henry. He hadn't had a panic attack in awhile. Now he just fainted every once in awhile when things seemed "mountain" difficult. Like, as difficult as a mountain. Still, he was really smart and my friend, even though he was a noob sometimes.

I leaned more against him and closed my eyes.

And, in a Minecraft flying machine high above the Earth, I fell asleep.

16

Steve was asleep in Minecraft, but he heard someone knocking loudly on his door. He put his pillow over his head and tried to continue sleeping, but then he heard a voice yelling through the door: it was Alex. Alex was one of his best friends.

She sounded angry.

Steve realized that she must have figured out that Herobrine had escaped the game and gone to Earth. Steve got out of bed and groggily rubbed his eyes.

He could hear Alex yelling: "Steve, something horrible has happened!"

Steve slowly walked to the door. He didn't want to have this conversation. Taking a deep breath, he opened the door.

"Herobrine is in Earth and he's going to destroy it," Alex said. "I just heard the news."

Steve sunk his head.

"Wait, did you know?" Alex asked.

She could tell by his reaction that he'd already known. She knew him really well since they'd been friends since childhood.

Steve knew he wouldn't have been able to hide the truth from her. "Yeah, I knew."

Alex immediately punched him in the chest. "What's wrong with you? Why didn't you tell me? How long have you known?"

"I can see that you're angry," said Steve. "But—"

"No," she interrupted. "We have to do something about this. We need to get to Earth and save them."

"How would we do that?" asked Steve. "I don't know how to cross over to Earth. Do you?"

She lowered her eyes. "No. But if Herobrine figured out a way. Then we could too."

"Even if we could," said Steve. "I don't see how we can stop Herobrine. He's impossible to stop."

"He used to be our friend. Maybe he would remember us."

Steve shook his head. "His mind has been twisted by evil."

Alex punched Steve in the arm once more. "Why didn't you tell me?"

"Because I knew that you would want to do something about it. But there's nothing we can do."

"That's a horrible attitude, Steve. We need to fight Herobrine. We need to figure out a way to fight him. He's going to destroy their planet and you know it."

Steve shrugged. "I know. It makes me really sad, but what can we do?"

"We can fight!"

"How?"

Alex shrugged.

"Look," said Steve, "I have friends on Earth." Steve

thought about Stevi, Henry and Jessica. They'd all become good friends the first time Steve was on Earth— but he'd gotten to Earth the first time because of a random glitch. "I wish I could save them," said Steve, getting tears in his eyes.

He looked down. Because there was nothing he could do.

Alex walked out the door, angry.

"Where are you going?" Steve asked.

"I'm going to figure out how to get to Earth."

Steve closed the door and went back to his bed and sat on the end of it. He wanted to cry or punch something. How could Herobrine be doing this to Earth?

But he knew there was no hope.

There was nothing he could do.

He didn't know how to get to Earth.

But he did know that Herobrine was unstoppable.

17

I woke up because the hot morning sun was blazing in through the glass block windows surrounding us. This was the bad thing about a glass flying machine. It was good at night, but it was really hot right now. My head was sweating, and Henry's hair was sticky and sweating onto me.

I shook him. "Wake up."

Larissa was awake. The three men were snoring. The rest of the boys were asleep. Henry slowly woke up, and I shook him some more.

"It's morning," I said.

He rubbed his eyes.

Beneath us was a crazy sight—there weren't any neighborhoods or streetlights or stadiums. There was just a bunch of green jungle, miles and miles of it, for as far as the eye could see.

"Are we there?" I asked Larissa.

She nodded. "About an hour away."

"We'll need to go mining," I said. "And gather supplies so we can fight Herobrine."

"We will," she said. "You should try to sleep more until we get there."

I closed my eyes again. That was probably a good idea. Henry wasn't ready to wake up anyway. We both went right back to sleep.

18

When I opened my eyes again, we were almost there. I knew we were almost there because we were going much slower. And we were much closer to the ground—it was only a few hundred feet beneath us rather than a few thousand feet beneath us.

I saw the three Zacks and Edwin were already awake and had climbed outside of the glass. They were on top of the flying machine, enjoying the strong wind.

It was hotter in here than ever and my hair was really sweaty. All the adults were awake now. I shook Henry awake.

"We're about here," said Larissa with a big smile.

"We're in South America?" I asked, to be sure.

"Yes, we are, sweetie!"

Larissa smiled really wide. She was really happy, apparently. Which I thought was weird. After all, we were about to fight Herobrine. It seemed like we should be fearful and quiet, not happy and smiley.

I looked at the Minecraft chest in the corner of the room, then up to Larissa. "What's next? When do we get supplies?"

"Soon. First we have to land in our secret underground cavern base."

That sounded cool.

"We're almost there," she added.

Henry was all the way awake now. "Is there food there?" he asked.

"Lotsa food," said Larissa. "Pancakes, eggs, bacon, toast, orange juice, all kinds of jellies."

Henry smiled to himself, and remained quiet.

He wasn't a morning person, but he always loved eating. I didn't like eating that much myself. It always took time away from playing handball, soccer, four square and, most of all, Minecraft.

But right now I was pretty hungry, and I figured it would be best to fight Herobrine on a full stomach. Pancakes sounded really good.

When I pictured the pancakes in my mind, my stomach made a really loud growling noise. "Excuse me," I said. And Henry and I laughed.

I saw that Edwin and the Zacharies were all up top jumping around on the glass. Minecraft glass is strong so there was no way they'd break it just from jumping. They were getting really close to the edges. For a moment, I thought one of them might fall off, which was scary because they would literally die. But none of them fell.

One of the three white suited men was flying the machine. He called out: "We're lowering. Approaching the destination."

Suddenly, I was more nervous than ever.

19

We were lowering even closer to the ground. I looked through the glass in all directions—it was all jungles and mountains. I even saw some ancient ruins—like old temples—dotted here and there throughout the large land. I couldn't see any houses or any people. Maybe some of them were hidden under the trees or something.

Then we flew over the top of a large hole in the ground —it was like a canyon. Sort of like the Grand Canyon, but obviously not as big.

The pilot of our flying machine stopped above the canyon and began lowering us to the ground. Apparently the secret base was down there.

Since we were still pretty high up, it took a long time to lower. After ten minutes, we finally reached the top of the canyon and then we began lowering inside of it. The walls surrounded us on each side as we got lower.

After five more minutes, our flying machine touched the ground at the bottom of the canyon. There were trees all around down here, but they were broken in pieces and scattered everywhere. Some of them were broken in complete half. It was a mess down here.

"We're here," said Larissa, happily.

Edwin and the Zacks jumped off the machine to the ground. They all picked up sticks first thing and began whacking each other with them.

Larissa motioned to Henry and I. "After you," she said.

I let Henry go first. We climbed onto the roof of the flying machine and then jumped down onto the floor. The moment my feet hit the ground, the flying machine lifted off the floor and burst into the air. Before any of us could react or try to do something, it was beyond our reach.

"What?" murmured Henry, confused.

All the adults were still in the machine, and they'd left us.

"Did they ditch us?" yelled Zack 3.

I looked all around. This canyon was giant. The flying machine was almost out of it. We could try to climb the walls to get out but they were so tall it would probably take us a day to reach the top. An entire day! And it looked incredibly dangerous. I looked all around, at all the broken trees, and I finally realized. This canyon wasn't normal. It wasn't a naturally generated canyon like the Grand Canyon.

It looked exactly like one of those types of giant holes that Herobrine makes in Minecraft.

I looked to Henry to tell him, but he already realized and spoke before I could. "Herobrine."

The other boys were too dumb to realize what was happening, plus they didn't play Minecraft. I looked around in every direction, looking for Herobrine. He wasn't anywhere to be seen and the day seemed very calm and pleasant.

But my heart was beating really fast.

I realized that the adults had trapped us. I didn't know why—but they'd flown us down here and left us for dead. Herobrine would be here soon. And since we didn't have any weapons or armor or potions or really ANYTHING —he would kill us all.

20

"Wait, what's happening?" said Edwin. "Why did they ditch us?"

"It was a trap all along," I said. "They delivered us to Herobrine."

"That's why they were acting so weird," said Henry. "Herobrine must have been mind-controlling them."

"That would make sense," I said.

That's why that guy kept making sheep noises and Larissa was so weird. Herobrine was controlling their minds and he wasn't doing a perfect job.

"We fell for it," said Henry. "They were probably real Minecraft game makers, but they were under Herobrine's mind control."

I finally realized the truth.

The official Minecraft game makers and programmers would have never recruited Henry and I to fight Herobrine. We were just kids. They would have gotten the army or something like I'd suggested earlier.

Herobrine had tricked us.

But why did Herobrine want to kill us?

I asked Henry, and he shrugged.

We were looking around toward the top of the canyon. The flying machine was far out of sight. I was scared we'd see Herobrine fly into the canyon. Any moment now.

If you don't know Herobrine, he sometimes makes gigantic pits like this one. He has all kinds of crazy powers. He can throw around rocks, he can create giant pits—he is basically an arbiter of destruction. He's really good at destroying things. That's his speciality. It's what he does.

Henry looked at me. "What are we going to do, Stevi?"

I didn't know.

Episode 2

1

"Where's the hidden base?" asked Edwin.

He didn't get it.

"There is no hidden base," I yelled, angry.

"What do you mean?"

"We were kidnapped and left here to be killed by Herobrine."

Edwin was really confused. "You mean, you brought us here to be eaten?"

"I don't think Herobrine eats people," said Henry.

"You brought us here to be killed?" he asked, angry.

"I didn't know that's what they were going to do with us," I said. "They ditched us down here to be killed by Herobrine."

"Why?"

I shrugged.

Just in case you're reading this and you forgot what happened in Episode 1 of "Herobrine In Real Life," I'll fill you in on what happened and where we currently are.

Basically, I'd been having a normal day. My friends and I found a pond with some fish in it, and we decided to sneak out of our houses that night after our parents were asleep so that we could see who could catch the first fish.

I snuck out.

We all met at the pond, but before we could do much fishing, we were attacked by people in white suits. It turns out they worked for the Minecraft company. They were adults. I had already met one of them before. I thought they were dressed weird and were acting weird, but I listened to what they had to say.

Basically, they told me that Herobrine had figured out a way to get out of the Minecraft video game and into our world. And that they needed my help to kill Herobrine before he destroyed our entire planet—which was his plan.

I'm sure all the stuff about Herobrine is true, because we were right now standing in a giant pit created by Herobrine himself!

Anyway, they said they needed my help. I thought that was weird, because why wouldn't they just hire the army? Why me? But I decided to believe them. Which was a mistake.

Because they flew us down here to South America— where Herobrine currently was—and they told us we were going to a secret base. They dropped us off in this pit instead, and then they flew away in their flying machine. Basically, they ditched us and left us for dead.

Now, we were like fish in a barrel for Herobrine to come down and kill. He wasn't here yet. I wasn't sure when he was going to be here.

One thing I was sure of—he would be able to kill us very easily, because we had no weapons, no armor, nothing. All we had was some backpacks full of snacks and flashlights. We'd need more than that to fight Herobrine.

Edwin looked very afraid. "What do we do, Stevi?"

2

That was the main question. And they were all looking at me now, waiting for my directions. They made me the leader in this moment. Probably because I knew the most about Minecraft. And probably because I saved our school from the wither boss last year.

I didn't know what to do.

Think, Stevi. Think.

We were somewhere in the middle-of-nowhere in South America so we couldn't count on anyone finding us or saving us. None of our parents knew where we were. None of us had cell phones with us and, even if we did, they wouldn't get reception out here in the middle of the jungle!

Henry was looking at me with his sheep eyes. He was very nervous right now. The three Zacks looked really confused. One was sucking his thumb. One was scratching his head. And one was sitting down looking at the ground and breathing heavily. Edwin crossed his arms and looked angry, like it was my fault for getting us into this situation.

And then there was me.

I was really confused about why Herobrine would want us. There was no reason he would want us, right? I'd never met him before. I had never even played against him in the game. I was really scared of him. He didn't know me.

It didn't make sense.

Maybe it was a mistake. Maybe the adults didn't mean to ditch us. Maybe the flying machine broke and took them up to the sky—but they'd be back down soon.

I knew that that was wishful thinking. They had really and truly ditched us and they weren't coming back. We'd probably never see them again.

I was shaking in fear, because I was really afraid of Herobrine, and I wasn't ready to fight him. I looked around at the canyon walls. They were too tall to climb. Herobrine would probably be here any minute. It would take us all day to climb the walls.

Think, Stevi.

And I finally realized. We needed to dig. We needed to go underground. We didn't have shovels or pickaxes or anything. We'd have to use our hands, which would take forever. But it was the only thing we could do.

3

"We have to dig!" I said.

"How?" said Henry. "We don't have—"

"With our hands."

"That'll take forever."

I ignored him. I already knew it would take forever, but what other choice did we have?

"I hate Minecraft," said Edwin. "Every time Minecraft comes into the real world, we have to work."

"Oh, shut up," I said. "We all need to dig."

I was already looking around for a good spot. I took off running to my right, and they all started following. I was going to the lowest spot in the canyon, figured that would be the closest to a potential mine or underground ravine. Or maybe there was a cave or pathway already.

I saw a spot that looked good for digging, but there were a lot of giant fallen trees in the way. This would be a difficult task.

"Stevi, I really don't want to dig," I heard Edwin saying.

But I ignored him and kept going towards the spot.

"Cave," Henry yelled. I looked around but didn't see it. Then I turned around, looked at him, saw where he was pointing.

He may have been right. In the distance, about twenty-five yards off to our right, was what looked like a cave entrance. I headed for it. They followed.

There was a ton of fallen trees in the path. I had to jump over tree trunks. Then there were some trunks that were too big. I had to climb onto them and jump off of them. I was going as fast as I could and my friends probably were too but they hadn't caught up to me yet. There was a lot of misshapen rocks down here. I ran up a rock, then jumped from it to a tree trunk. Then jumped from that tree trunk to another one. I landed perfectly and then jumped off onto the ground.

Almost to the cave entrance.

That's when we all heard a loud bass noise that sounded like it was coming from above, like thunder, and it reverberated throughout the whole canyon, bouncing around the canyon walls.

It wasn't thunder, though—it was growling.

I turned around and tilted my head back. Herobrine was there, hovering directly above the center of the canyon. He was pretty high up, but I could see his bright white eyes.

They were looking right at me.

4

"He—he—he—Herobrine!" Henry stuttered.

"To the cave," I yelled.

And we all continued running. I jumped onto a tree trunk, but it was slippery and I almost fell. I got both feet on it and turned, waiting for Henry and the others to catch up to me.

Henry reached me in about five seconds. I grabbed his hand and pulled him onto the trunk. Now Edwin and the others were here.

The ground started shaking beneath us as if an earthquake was happening. It was Herobrine. He had the powers to destroy the ground. He was shaking it.

I jumped off the trunk and landed on the ground, which was rolling like an ocean wave. It threw me off my feet. I landed on my elbow and knee, scraping them pretty bad.

But I crawled forward, getting to my feet on the rolling ground, which was making my stomach queazy. I had to jump over the waves as they came at me.

The problem was—we were on a patch of dirt. The

next tree trunks were about fifteen feet in front of us. As the waves rolled toward us, we jumped over them and it wasn't that hard. But somehow we had to get over the rolling waves where the tree trunks were. The waves were kicking up the tree trunks into the air.

Then I realized, we could try to dive underneath them. But we would have to get to the other side before they fell back down on top of us and CRUSHED us!

I made it to the first trunk.

We were all standing side by side before it, watching it pop up and down. Henry was very nervous, I could tell. But I didn't look at him. I waited for the trunk to pop into the air. Then I dove under it and rolled forward. The tree trunk fell down behind me, slightly touching my back. I'd made it! I wondered if all the rest of them would be able to do that, though.

The cave entrance was right there—only fifteen feet in front of me.

But I realized that we were wrong. It wasn't a cave entrance. It was blocked in by stone. From further away, it had looked like a cave. But it wasn't.

It didn't matter anyway.

Right then, Herobrine destroyed the floor beneath us. With a giant crashing noise, the stone and dirt crumbled under our feet and began to disappear to pieces and shards.

I heard tree trunks snapping in half and branches breaking. Twigs started hitting me, and small rocks and pebbles. One stick hit me in the face really hard. I was afraid one of my eyes would get poked out.

And then we were all falling down and down into the new pit Herobrine was creating, with rocks falling with us,

all around us.
   I didn't know if we'd survive.

We were all SCREAMING!

Zack 3 was screaming like a little girl. I couldn't help myself. I was a girl. We fell and fell and fell through the air, and I knew we were going to die.

But then the ground stopped breaking.

I landed on my feet on a tree trunk. It bounced against the floor and launched me upward about ten feet. I flailed my arms around, trying to stay straight up and down in the air so I could land back down on my feet.

Whoosh!

I fell back to the floor and landed on my feet.

I looked all around and saw Henry laying on the floor. He looked hurt. I ran over to him to see if he was okay. And I heard Herobrine let out another giant growl.

6

Henry was moaning there, on the floor. I couldn't hear him that well because Herobrine was growling and he was much closer to us. I looked up and saw him descending into the pit.

I got beside Henry and rolled him over so I could see his face. He had blood coming out of his nose. "Oh, Henry!" I yelled. "Are you okay?"

He rubbed his nose and then rubbed his eyes—rubbing blood all around his eyes. He blinked a lot. He didn't answer me. But he did look over to his right and point his arm.

I looked over and saw a REAL CAVE ENTRANCE.

It was right there, about fifteen feet away.

I looked around and saw Edwin getting to his feet and dusting himself off. He looked up at Herobrine and yelled, "Go away!"

Herobrine growled and the ground started rumbling again.

We needed to get into that cave.

I saw the Zacks in various places, getting to their feet.

They seemed to be okay. And the ground was rumbling but it hadn't started rolling yet. Which meant we had a little bit of time.

"Over here! Hurry!"

I pulled Henry to his feet. He took a step and almost fell over from being dizzy. I held him up. "I'm okay now," he said.

And we ran for the cave entrance.

We were a few feet away when the ground started rolling. Herobrine was too late this time. The entrance, which he had accidentally created, was two blocks high. I ran into it first and saw that it was a stairway tunnel, descended downwards.

It was really cool looking.

This is how it was last time Minecraft came into real life. Basically, our world changed a tiny bit to be more like Minecraft. Everything still looks the same, but stone and dirt react as if they are apart of Minecraft. Basically, our world becomes like Minecraft but with an Earth texture pack. Everything looked exactly like Earth, but you could dig out blocks and create diamond swords. Which is what we would do if we could find diamonds fast enough.

Right now, our only priority was to get away from Herobrine!

I ran down the stairs, jumping down one block at a time. Then I came to a step that went three blocks down. Didn't hesitate. I jumped down, landed on my feet and bent my knees—which is the proper way to jump off of stuff.

The guys were all behind me.

The Earth was shaking all around us.

"It's going to cave in over our heads," I heard Edwin

yelling.

I looked up as I continued running. The ceiling was shaking and small pebbles and dirt was falling from it. He was right. But this stairway might lead us to somewhere safe.

A big rock fell in front of me.

I jumped over it and kept running.

One problem: as we continued down the stairway it started getting really dark. It started becoming hard for me to see more than a few feet ahead.

We didn't have torches!

Then I remembered—we had flashlights.

I didn't have time to get mine out of the backpack, though. We needed to keep running before the ceiling broke over our heads and we got crushed by heavy rocks.

"Stevi!" Henry yelled out of fear.

"Keep running!" I yelled.

7

Enderman noises.

I could hear them, which was surprising because everything was so loud what with Herobrine's giant growling noises and the ceiling shaking and about to cave in on us.

I heard that scratchy scary noise that Endermen make.

I saw that the tunnel stairway we were in widened out on each side of us. But it was dark and I couldn't see much. I kept my head straight forward.

I realized another problem: the 3 Zacks and Edwin didn't play Minecraft and didn't know much about it. They wouldn't know that you're not supposed to look into an Enderman's eyes. You know, because they'll kill you!

I didn't know how to explain it to them now. Even if I yelled, everything had gotten so loud that they probably wouldn't be able to hear me. So I kept running down the tunnel, jumping down the one and two block steps, hoping that we would somehow get out of this.

Herobrine had lured us into this giant pit to kill us.

As I ran, I thought about how we didn't fall that far

when he'd destroyed the ground beneath our feet. Normally, if I knew my Minecraft correctly (and I'm a professional at Minecraft), he created much bigger pits. Then I remembered how when Steve first came into our world he had had a hard time speaking and moving. He glitched out a little bit as he got used to living in our world.

Maybe Herobrine, because he was new to our world, didn't have full strength yet. Maybe he glitched out—which bode well for us. Gave us chance.

Maybe.

And maybe that's why he was growling so much instead of talking and speaking to us with actual words. Or maybe he was growling because he was Herobrine and he was EVIL and CRAZY.

Yeah, probably the second part.

Still, I didn't think he was at full strength yet.

I heard more Endermen noises.

Then I remembered. Since Minecraft was in real life again, there would be a lot of dangerous mobs down here. If a creeper showed up from the darkness and exploded, we'd all die. None of us had armor.

I decided to stop thinking all these things. Thinking of these fears wouldn't help us escape and beat Herobrine. We needed to run even faster. That's what I focused on.

I ran as hard as I possibly could.

I jumped off a three block step, then ran forward. The tunnel was flat here. The stairway ended. And I saw light up ahead. I ran to the end of the tunnel and stopped because it ended in a cliff. I peered down the cliff. It was a little bit brighter around here because there were patches of lava far down below, scattered here and there.

The cliff was pretty tall—over one hundred blocks.

And we'd found a RAVINE!

This was perfect. Sure, there were patches of lava, including one directly beneath us, but there was also a river running down the middle of the ravine. We could run and jump off this cliff. If we jumped far enough, we'd make it over the lava and land in the water.

It would be dangerous, but I knew we could do it.

Besides we had no other choice.

The boys were around me now, looking down.

"We have to jump the lava, into the water," I yelled over the noise of the ceiling rumbling and Herobrine's evil growls.

Henry was nodding. He knew it was our only choice.

Edwin was breathing heavily. "How?"

"We have to," I yelled, stepping back, away from the cliff. "I'll go first. But you guys better go after me, because if you don't, you'll probably die."

They made a part for me so that I could run.

I backed up more than ten feet. Dirt was falling onto my head and Herobrine was louder than ever. We didn't have much more time.

I ran as fast as I could.

I reached the edge of the cliff and jumped off of my right foot as hard as I could, and then I was flying through the air—and then falling. It was a long fall.

I wasn't sure if I'd make it past the lava.

8

A few seconds went by as I fell through the air, and I realized that I was going to make it. I'd jumped far enough out that I was going to land in the WATER.

I only hoped the boys wouldn't be scared. If they hesitated and didn't jump, they probably would die. If they jumped and made it to the water, then we could all swim under the water and hold our breath as the roof caved. We had more chances in the ravine.

SPLASH!

I landed in the water, and it didn't hurt one bit. I swam out of the way so the next person wouldn't land on my head. Zack 2 landed down in the water with a splash. Then Edwin.

Henry was really scared. He had wanted to jump right after Stevi, but he was letting the other boys go first because he was better at Minecraft. He'd already survived a real life mining mission before. So had Edwin, technically, but Edwin was a scaredy-cat even though he acted tough.

Zack 3 jumped.

Zack 1 was the only one left.

That's when an Enderman popped right in front of them, blocking them from being able to jump off the cliff. Zack 1 had never seen an Enderman before and he yelled in terror.

Henry grabbed Zack's hand and ran toward the Enderman, keeping his head down, being sure not to look at the very tall and scary creature.

"Don't look at him," Henry yelled, but he wasn't sure if Zack was listening.

Henry ran at the Enderman, then ran right into him.

The Enderman got mad and pushed the two boys backwards, throwing them into the nearest wall. Henry and Zack fell to the ground on their shoulders—hard.

With a giant snapping noise—which sounded very thunderous and explosive—the ceiling above them began to cave inward.

It didn't seem like Henry and Zack had much of a chance.

9

The Enderman, just as he had popped into the world randomly, popped out of the world. Giant rocks were falling in from the ceiling, down towards Henry and Zack.

Henry grabbed Zack by the arm and, with all his might, yanked him forward. Zack understood what was happening and they ran toward the cliff's edge.

A giant rock that would have crushed them fell right behind them. They were at the edge of the cliff and it started to break. They jumped off at the last moment and began the long fall downwards.

They just barely missed the lava, landed softly in the water.

The others were all here, looking up, watching the giant rocks fall towards them. The river here was more than one block deep—and that was why Stevi had known it was a good idea to jump down here.

I saw Henry and Zack barely make it into the water.

"Everyone under," I yelled. "Swim down as deep as you can."

That said, I took a deep breath and dove under the water and swam as fast and hard as I could. It was a pretty deep river, which was a good thing.

I opened my eyes under the water.

It was bright under here because of the lava blocks that were close by. I could see all of us down here, looking at one another, and looking up. Giant rocks and boulders and tree trunks splashed into the water over our heads.

The water slowed their fall, but they sank pretty fast in the water. We had to swim out of the way. We watched the big objects fall toward us and we dodged them.

A giant boulder nearly fell on Henry, but I grabbed his hand and yanked him out of the way. Finally, after a good forty-five seconds, the objects stopped hitting the water. We'd survived Herobrine's second attack. But I knew he would try to get us again.

I swam out of the way of a falling tree trunk, and I started to realize something. There were two reasons that we were still alive: either Herobrine wasn't as strong as usual because he wasn't accustomed to Earth yet, or he wasn't trying to kill us. Maybe he was just trying to scare us and get us on the run.

I didn't know why I'd had that second thought, because it didn't make any sense. Herobrine was very evil. Why would he only try to scare us?

I swam towards the surface of the water, and saw out of the corner of my eyes that my friends were doing the same. I came out of the water and breathed in the cave air. It was a little smelly—like coal or gun powder. That's when I heard the noise of a creeper.

I looked toward the noise.

On the embankment of the river, only a few blocks

away, was a giant creeper. These things were so much larger in real life than I was used to. In the game, they were pretty scary—especially when you don't have armor of any kind, and especially when they sneak up on you.

In real life, they were so tall.

This one was much taller than I—triple my size.

And he was already buzzing, preparing to explode.

He jumped into the water to swim toward us.

On top of this new development, I looked up and saw gaping holes in what used to be the ceiling over us. And I saw Herobrine descending through one of the holes.

A creeper coming towards us and Herobrine entering the cavern!

"Swim!" I said.

10

I wasn't sure if Edwin and the three Zacks even knew about creepers and that they freakin' exploded. But they were swimming away from the giant thing. It was really scary looking, so I guess no explanation was needed.

We swam as fast as we could, but there was a lot of big rocks and tree trunks in our way. We had to try to climb over them in the water, and swim around them.

We were all splashing hard, trying to get out of there.

There was a giant boulder that I was able to stand on. I ran to the other end of it and jumped over a log, back into the water.

That's when Herobrine's powerful growl filled the air in the cavern. It sounded even louder down here because the growl echoed. It made the Zacks scream in terror.

And then the creeper blew up behind us.

It sent shreds of logs toward us, and it created a giant splash in the water which landed all over us. I kept swimming for a few more moments, realizing I was okay —I'd been out of the blast zone. I turned around and saw my friends were okay as well.

"Keep swimming!" I yelled.

That's when the floor beneath us, beneath the river, started rumbling. This was bad. Herobrine was going to cause another earthquake and destroy the ground beneath us.

The ground started rolling.

It might have been just me, but it felt even more powerful this time. As if he were getting stronger. The river was at least thirty blocks wide. Which was nice.

And the water started creating waves.

They started small, like ripples.

But then they grew, and now the water was splashing against each bank, splashing each way. The waves grew bigger and bigger and it made it hard to swim and tread water.

Luckily my friends knew how to swim.

Herobrine was becoming more violent.

He was definitely getting stronger.

There was a lot more light in here since the ceiling was opened up in a lot of places. The mid-morning sun was blasting in through certain places, creating giant shafts of bright white light. I swam through a section of it, and it was really hot.

Then I was in the shade again. The waves were crashing against the sides of the river, sending water up a good twenty feet into the air. Any moment now and Herobrine would break the ground beneath us.

And then, with a giant growl, he did.

11

We would need a miracle to survive this.

All of the boys were yelling. I wasn't. Because I wasn't sure what to think. I wasn't sure what to do. I wasn't sure how we could survive Herobrine.

12

GIANT WAVES!

The water was splashing violently everywhere. This whole underground world was in chaos, and I could barely tell what was happening.

The water sucked me down under and then pulled me a certain direction. I put my hands out over my head to hopefully stop myself from crashing into anything—like a boulder or maybe the side wall of the river or maybe one of my friends.

I needed to protect my head.

My eyes were closed, on instinct.

But I opened them. I could barely see under the water, because a few boulders had blocked the path of the lava light for the moment. Also there were bubbles everywhere from the water being shaken up so much.

That's when a giant rock—it could definitely be called a boulder—fell on me and began taking me down to the bottom of the river. I looked and could see the floor of the river was close. The rock was going to crush me into the floor.

I tried swimming away from it, peeling off the rock, but I was stuck to it. It was sinking too fast and gravity had me STUCK to it!

13

Henry's body was flipping around in circles in the water, rolling every which way. He curled up in a ball and put his hands over his head. It was good he did, because his head rammed into something, and it was slightly protected from his hands.

He couldn't stay curled—not after smacking so hard into something.

He realized it was the river's side wall.

His fingers were hurting because they'd been crushed, basically.

He opened and closed his hands to make sure they were okay—they were. They only hurt really bad. And then the water was carrying him downstream, really fast. He clambered about, trying to get to the surface, but waves covered him and covered him.

He was running out of breath.

He broke to the surface of the water for a moment and heard two of the boys screaming—he couldn't tell which ones. He took a quick breath. And then the water covered him again.

This was very bad.
If they survived this, it would be pure luck or a miracle.

14

Steve was on a walk. Alex was right. He had to try to do something. He couldn't just lounge around his house hoping that the Earth people would figure out how to stop Herobrine. They wouldn't be able to stop Herobrine with tanks or even nuclear bombs. In order to fight Minecraft mobs, you have to use Minecraft stuff—you have to use potions, enchanted diamond swords and armor. You have to be pro at Minecraft. And by the time the world realized you had to fight Minecraft with Minecraft, it would probably be too late—and probably a lot of innocent people would be dead.

Steve had to figure out a way into Earth.

But how?

Alex was trying to figure out a way.

He needed to find Alex, even though she was mad at him. He would need her help to defeat Herobrine if they did figure out a way to get to Earth.

Also, two minds were better than one, and Alex was really smart. Maybe even smarter than him. He changed the direction he was walking—started going toward Alex's house.

15

I was stuck to the rock and was only a few feet away from crashing into the ground. I would be crushed like a pancake. I pictured myself looking like a pancake and it made me want to throw up. I almost lost my breath. I lost a little bit of it, which was bad, because I needed to hold my breath as long as I could. I suppose, though, it didn't matter how much breath I had if I was going to be crushed like a pancake.

16

I was basically stuck to the bottom of the rock, and couldn't get away from it fast enough. When I was only five feet away from the floor of the ravine, I accidentally let go of the breath I was holding because I was screaming!

But right then the rock stopped.

It stopped falling!

I realized that it was too wide—it got stuck against the sides of the ravine.

There was a small one foot gap for me to swim through—easy. Then I was free. I swam as fast as I could back to the surface so I could breathe.

I broke through the surface and took a gigantic breath, whipping my head around everywhere to see what was happening.

I noticed a few things.

One—Herobrine was midway down into this cavern, really close to us.

Two—the cave-in and earthquake was over.

Things were calm again.

Three—all my friends were still alive. Edwin was on top of a rock. Henry was on top of a giant log that criss-crossed the top of the river.

For the moment, things were calm.

But I knew Herobrine would create another earthquake.

That's when I heard a sizzling noise coming from behind me. I turned around and saw that a big pool of lava had been broken up and the lava was seeping into the river.

Once it hit the river, it was very quickly being carried down towards us.

Immediately, I began swimming away from it. There was so much junk clogging up the river right here that I had to swim under logs, climb over logs.

"Swim!" I yelled to my friends.

I looked back and saw that even more lava was entering the river. This was insane! We were running away from lava!

That's when Herobrine started shaking the ground—AGAIN.

There was a big rock in my way. I had to climb onto it. It was slippery and I couldn't find a place to hold it to pull myself up. That's when Zack 2 appeared on top of the rock and gave me his hand. He helped me up. Once I was standing on the rock, I saw something down the river.

A boat!

But it wasn't just a boat. There was a girl in the boat.

I wondered if this was our miracle—because, as I'd said, we needed a miracle to escape. The girl and the boat was down a ways, about two hundred feet. The cave-in hadn't happened over there and the river was flowing nice and evenly. Her boat was tied up to a rock off to the side, keeping her in place. She was standing up in the boat, watching us.

Even though the lighting was dim where she was, I could see all of this clearly. And Zack 2 was looking as well. "She has a boat!" he yelled

The rest of my friends were noticing as well.

Henry yelled: "She could save us!"

He was right. Her boat wasn't the typical one-person type of Minecraft boat. It was a human boat—big enough for all of them to fit. It had oars on either side of it. I did notice she had a Minecraft chest in the boat. Which meant she was a human here on Earth who had figured out that Minecraft had come to Earth and she was mining to make Minecraft weapons.

"To the boat!" I yelled.

The ground was shaking even more and the water started splashing up again on all sides as we scrambled over the tops of rocks and trees and rocks and sticks, away from the flowing lava that was still coming towards us.

Finally, I got past all the debris and was in the open and clear water. I turned around, swimming backwards, and watched my friends jump over and swim under the last bits of blockage in the water. Then they were swimming after me. That's when Herobrine broke the ground once more.

17

I yelled as loud as I could one last time: "Get to the boat!"

I didn't know if I was yelling it for myself or for the others, because there was no way they could have heard me. Herobrine's growl was louder than ever and the sound of stone and wood and dirt blocks breaking into pieces was like the sound of an explosion.

Plus the water was sloshing around as if someone had thrown a bomb into it. The waves were everywhere, the water was trying to push me down. I paddled with my arms as hard as I could, trying to take breaths when I could—when I wasn't being pushed under the water.

I took a big breath, then purposely dove under the water and swam down, away from all the new falling rocks and trees. I swam as hard as I could.

And I noticed something—a good sign.

Herobrine had messed up.

However he'd broken the ground this time, he had forced the water to move more violently downstream. What did this mean?—

That swimming towards the boat was super easy because the current was helping us. I was swimming hard, and the current was helping me super much. I was going super fast. I saw Henry underwater off to my right, and the three Zacks and Edwin off to my left.

Rocks were falling into the water over us, but it didn't matter, because the current was super strong—like a river of rapids—and it was carrying us downriver, towards the boat.

We'd make it to the boat in seconds rather than minutes.

Then I remembered the lava.

If the water was moving faster, then the lava would be moving faster as well. I didn't stop swimming, but I glanced behind me. The lava was about fifteen feet away, and it was coming for us—FAST.

18

My friends hadn't noticed the lava, but they were still swimming forward as fast as they could, so it didn't matter. Edwin and the Zacks were actually in front of me. They were probably better swimmers, which I hated to admit.

Henry was lagging behind.

I pictured the lava touching poor Henry's legs and burning him, and it was a horrific thought. I swam towards him. When I got to him, I grabbed his arm and pulled him forward with me. He'd been making one mistake, though it wasn't his fault. The current was stronger in the center of the river and he'd been swimming along the outside.

I pulled him into the center of the river and we gained more speed. I glanced back again and saw the lava was even closer.

I also could see from here that Edwin and the others were swimming toward the surface. I looked to the surface and saw the boat was there!

Henry and I began pulling for the surface.

A giant boulder fell in our way. It was massive, probably the biggest one so far, and it looked like it was going to block our way.

We couldn't go under it because it would crush us. It was falling too fast. We couldn't go over it because it was too tall.

The lava was catching up to us.

The current threw us right into the boulder, and we got stopped against it. I realized what we had to do. We started swimming for the side of the river. We had to get up on the bank before the lava reached us. The current was trying to pin us against the boulder, but we fought for the bank. We swam and even found some handholds on the rock to pull ourselves toward the embankment.

Just as the lava reached us, Henry got onto the bank, grabbed my hand, and pulled me out of the water. Then we ran for the boat. The boys were climbing into it as we ran.

The girl saw Henry and I and yelled, "Is that all of you?"

"Yes!" I said.

"Get in!" she yelled.

She had a sword in her hand and was standing by the rope. Henry and I ran down the bank—rocks were still falling everywhere. I didn't dare look back.

Henry was in front of me and he dove from the embankment to the boat. I dove right after him. We both landed on the hard wood, and right then, the girl cut the rope with her sword. Since there was a current, the boat immediately started going down the river. The girl jumped in the boat.

Then we were rolling down the river SUPER FAST—it

was as if we were on a river raft in rapid water. I saw the water had whitecaps here and there—which basically meant the river was going really fast.

I looked back and saw Herobrine was still in the cave, just watching us with his glowing eyes. He'd failed so far. Was he going to come after us?

I saw rocks and trees still falling into the river behind us. I saw the lava seeping past the giant boulder that had fallen in mine and Henry's way.

Then I sat down in the boat and took hold of an oar. Henry did as well. The others followed. We started paddling, making ourselves go even faster! We were probably going thirty miles per hour! Maybe more.

Herobrine got further and further away by the moment. He wasn't flying after us. The rocks weren't falling down where we were. We rowed and rowed and rowed. And after two minutes I realized that we were safe.

We entered a place in the river where there were no lava pits, and it went completely pitch dark. We stopped rowing, and all we could hear was the sound of the rushing water and our boat being carried very fast down the river—the rudder was slicing through the water, creating a wake out the back of the boat. I could see the wake slightly in the darkness because it had white water in it.

All the sudden I began wondering: were we safe? Was Herobrine going to come after us? Did we win? And who was this girl?

19

The darkness didn't go away for a few minutes, and none of us really had anything to say. We just sat in our seats, without talking. We'd just been through A LOT.

I did hear Zack 3 fart twice, but luckily we were going so fast that I never smelled it.

Zack 1 was the first to speak. He yelled: "That. Was. AWESOME!"

20

There were a few lava pits up ahead, and we could finally see again. There were tall spiders—remember, in the Minecraft game, spiders and mobs don't always seem that threatening, but in real life they're giant and really scary. Also remember, we still had no armor.

Although the girl in the boat did—she had diamond feetings, but that was it. She also had an iron sword.

I watched the tall spiders hiss at us as we passed them. They didn't chase us. So that was good. Then I remembered that Herobrine could mind control mobs. He could mind control the spiders to attack us. You can tell when Herobrine is mind controlling a mob because their eyes turn white. But he wasn't mind controlling these spiders.

That was good.

I noticed that the water behind us was crystal clear. There was no lava in it. We were finally, for the moment, safe.

I was going to talk to the girl who had saved our lives, but the river ended up ahead. I started noticing there were more and more mobs back here.

I saw three creepers on a ledge above us. I saw more tall spiders walking around on the banks of the river. I was happy there weren't any skeletons.

But just as I thought it, an arrow landed right in the center of the boat with a giant THUD. The arrow stuck into the wood floor, and all the boys freaked out.

"We have to go down the water slides," said the girl who'd saved us.

"Water slides?" Henry asked, sounding nervous.

Henry was afraid of water slides.

"Yes," she said, pointing.

She was pointing at the wall where the river ended. Well, the river didn't end at the wall—it formed into a waterfall that went under the wall. I could tell that it was a tall waterfall because I couldn't hear the water crashing down from here.

There were holes in the wall here and there that looked like the entrances to water slides. They were natural water slides, formed into the rock.

Another arrow landed in the boat, only inches away from me.

I saw that there were multiple skeletons on stone walkways high above us. If we didn't abandon the boat, they would certainly kill us or wound us with arrows.

Our boat reached the wall.

The girl immediately got out and went to the nearest available water slide entrance. She jumped through it without saying another word.

Henry was really nervous.

"It'll be all right," I said, but I wasn't sure.

I went to one of the entrances and dove through head

first so that Henry could see I wasn't afraid, though I sort of was.

And the water slide was WILD!

Episode 3

1

Welcome to Episode 3 of "Herobrine In Real Life."

My name is Stevi, and things have gotten REAL. Literally, Minecraft has come into the real world, Earth. Our world. That part is great. The bad part is that Steve and Alex aren't here. Some cool mobs are here, I'm sure —like pigs, horses, and llamas.

But Herobrine is also here.

And his plan is to destroy the world.

In case you missed episode 1 and 2 of this story, here's basically what has happened. In episode 1, I explained how we were kidnapped by human people—adults—in white suits. They tricked us. They said they worked for Minecraft. And actually that part was probably true. But they were actually under a spell from Herobrine. He was mind controlling them.

They told us they needed my help to defeat Herobrine.

We got in their flying machine and flew down to South America, where Herobrine currently is, to try to destroy him. But then the white-suited people dropped us off in a giant pit (it was practically a canyon). It was a trap.

That was where episode 2 started.

In episode 2, Herobrine tried to kill us multiple times, but we escaped because we found an underground river, and then we found a mysterious girl who had a boat.

We barely escaped.

Though it seemed like Herobrine had given up and let us live.

We made it to the end of the river, where there were naturally formed rock water slides. That's where this book starts.

Enjoy the ride, because things get even crazier!

2

I had jumped into the waterslide headfirst. After about five seconds, I realized that had probably been a mistake, and I started screaming my head off!

The water slide shot STRAIGHT DOWN!

My body wasn't even touching the stone slide. I was falling straight down and down and down—like Alice In Wonderland. That girl may have accidentally sent us all to our deaths!

Then I had some hope because the slide started curving so that I was actually sliding on it. There was a lot of water shooting down the slide so it was a smooth ride, and the stone was nice and smooth, having been carved out and eroded over time by the water—*that's right, Mom and Dad, I pay attention in geology class. It's called erosion.*

The stone and water was really cold, but I was too excited to pay much attention to it. A lot of time went by of sliding and my fears went away. I was going really fast and it was really fun. The girl must have known these slides were good. I was sure she lived around these parts because she looked South American.

It was pitch dark here, just like a waterslide at a waterpark. There was no light, and the water was really echoey. "Awesome!" I yelled, and I heard my echo.

"Stevi!" I heard Henry yell from somewhere. He must have been in my slide—there had been multiple ones to choose from. He must have followed me.

"Henry!" I yelled back.

"This is awesome!" he yelled.

"I know!"

After two minutes of sliding—this was the greatest waterslide in the world!—it finally curved out until it was level. We slowed down a lot, but the water was still pushing us.

Finally we exited the slide into a giant open cave. We shot of out the slide into a bright pool of water. I looked around the cave—it was amazing.

The pool we were in was definitely man-made—there were a few lava blocks in the floor that made it nice and bright. And all around the lava blocks was diamond blocks—aligned symmetrically.

It was like something Henry and I built in Minecraft. We always like to make everything symmetrical and nice looking. The rest of the cave was just as amazing as the pool.

The girl had already made it down the slide. She was sitting at the edge of the pool.

"Who are you?" I asked. "And where are we?"

3

I swam to the edge of the pool and got out of it. That's when I realized how cold I was.

"I have towels over here," said the girl.

All the boys were climbing out of the pool and they were all accounted for: the 3 Zacks, Edwin, and Henry.

This cave was basically an underground base—it was like Batman's bat cave.

"Is this your base?" I asked the girl.

"Yes," she said.

She had a Brazilian accent.

There was a lot of cool stuff here. I saw a whole wall of Minecraft chests—they were labeled. Weapons. Food. Armor. Materials. Iron.

She was growing nether warts.

She went to a box and took out towels, handing them to each of us.

She'd decorated this place pretty nice. It wasn't very large, but she'd places torches here and there. There was a mine cart and a track that led out a tunnel, which was probably the way out.

"Who are you?" I asked.

"I'm Anna," she said. "Who are you?"

"I'm Stevi."

"You're white and you talk like an American."

"Yes. I am."

"What are you doing down here in Brazil?"

"Trying to kill Herobrine."

"You failed."

I nodded my head.

All the boys were drying off. Zack 3 was whipping his head around to get the water out of his hair like he was a dog or something. He sprayed water all over me.

"Gross," I said.

Anna laughed. "These are weird ones."

I told her all of their names.

Henry was standing by me now. "I'm Henry," he said, reaching out his hand.

They shook hands.

"You know how to play Minecraft?" I asked.

"Yes," she said.

"Did you get kidnapped from the white suit people?" I asked.

"No." She looked confused.

"Who are you, then?" I asked.

"My village was destroyed by Herobrine. Some of my friends died. I'm trying to destroy him now. Why are you trying to kill him? You look like you're only nine-years-old."

"I'm ten," I said. "And you look like you're only nine."

"I'm eleven," she said.

"We were tricked," I explained. "It's a long story."

"You want to help me kill him?" she asked.

"Yes. But I don't know if it's possible," I said.

She nodded, like she understood. "He is very powerful."

She looked very sad. Herobrine had killed some of her friends. I felt really bad for her. I couldn't imagine if Henry died. I would cry for days, probably years.

Anna sat down on the stone floor. I sat down too. We all sat, forming a circle. The three Zacks were the first to speak: "We're really hungry!"

"There's food over there," said Anna, pointing to the wall of chests.

They all ran over. "Which box?" they all yelled.

"The one that says 'Food' on it, dummies," yelled Anna.

"Ohhhhhhh."

Now it was just Edwin, Anna, Henry, and me.

"Do you know a lot about Minecraft?" Anna asked me.

"Yes."

"More than me?" she asked.

"How much have you played?" I asked.

"A lot. But mostly at my cousin's house. I also read some Minecraft books. I only get to play when I visit my cousin in the city. Mostly I live in the jungle in my village."

"I live in my room," I said. "Me and Henry play everyday."

"That's good," she said. "So how do we beat Herobrine?"

That was a good question.

Because I didn't know.

4

It was always difficult to think on an empty stomach, so I got up and got some steak from the box. Then I ate my steak, holding it in one hand, while I paced around the bat-like cave. I was glad my mom wasn't here to see me eating the steak with my hands, which is my preferred method of steak eating. It filled my health bars pretty quick. I mean, I know I don't have real health bars like Minecraft, but still. I felt a lot better. I hadn't eaten breakfast.

Henry ate chicken.

How could we beat Herobrine? *How could we beat Herobrine?* He was super powerful. He could fly. He could control mobs and humans.

But it didn't make sense.

Why hadn't he killed us? Surely, he had to be more powerful than that. We were humans with no armor or weapons, and he wasn't able to kill us. Or maybe he wasn't trying to kill us.

None of it made sense.

"I don't know how to beat him," I said.

"Neither do I," said Henry.

"We should punch him in the face," said Zack 1.

"We should stab him with something sharp," said Zack 2. "Like a sword. Or like a sharp blade of grass. I once poked myself with a sharp blade of grass and it hurt."

"Do you mean 'glass?'" I asked.

"Um, yeah. I think I mean 'glass.'" To himself, he muttered: "Was it *glass or grass?*"

Zack 3 farted.

"Gross," said Anna. "You look like you need a bath. You have a dirty face."

Zack 3 smiled.

"Ignore them," I said. "Henry and I know the most."

"I'm really smart too," Edwin said.

"Not really!" I said.

"I know a lot about Minecraft," he said.

"You don't even play."

"Sometimes I do."

"Name one diamond sword enchantment," I said.

"That doesn't even matter," he said. "I play it."

"Ignore him, too," I said.

Edwin was mad now. "Whatever, Stevi. You almost got us all killed! I was having a good day until I started hanging out with you. We almost got shot by those white suit people. And we almost got killed by the Herobrine monster. Because of YOU!"

He stormed away from us, to another side of the room, where he laid down to take a nap. Now it was just me, Anna, and Henry trying to figure it all out.

I started wondering if Edwin was right.

Was this all my fault?

It was, after all, dumb of me to believe the white suit

people.

"It's not your fault," said Henry. Henry then said to Anna, "She's the smartest Minecraft person I know. And she's my best friend."

"She's not your girlfriend?" Anna asked. "I thought she was."

"What?!" Henry explained. "No!"

"No, no, no," I said. "He's just my friend."

Anna smiled. "It sounds like you like each other."

"No way, Jose," I said.

"Jose says no," said Henry, mumbling. "No way."

"In that case," said Anna, stepping closer to Henry. "I think you're really cute, for an American boy."

Henry's face blushed. "I guess so."

"Do you like girls yet?" she asked.

Now Henry's face was BRIGHT red. "Well, yeah. But —but—but I live in America and you don't know my mom yet—"

I decided to save him, because he obviously was embarrassed by her and maybe even liked her. "We need to focus on Herobrine," I said.

Henry's face was still red. "I'm going to get more chicken," he said.

The honest truth right now was that everything was happening so fast. Just minutes ago we almost died from a Herobrine attack! Before that we were betrayed by Minecraft game makers. I didn't know what to think or do.

5

I needed some time alone to think. It was a small echoey cave so there wasn't many places I could go to be alone. I went and sat by the bright and shiny pool. I rolled up my jeans so that I could let my legs dangle into the water.

I could hear the 3 Zacks playing ninja. Edwin was sulking alone in a corner. And Henry was nervously talking to Anna.

I tried thinking of our options. The first thought that came to mind was that we could fight Herobrine. In order to fight him ourselves, we would need to do a lot of resource gathering. We would even have to go into the Nether and that seemed like a lot of work. Also, I wasn't sure if I could beat Herobrine. He was probably the greatest villain in all of Minecraft.

The Zacks didn't know much about Minecraft. Henry was right—Edwin was not to be trusted. And Anna seemed like she had skills.

Were we a good enough team to beat Herobrine?

Then I realized that another way to beat Herobrine

would probably be to access the Minecraft code. If we could change the Minecraft code, maybe we could send Herobrine back into the Minecraft game. That would be an easier way of doing it. But we would have to find a Minecraft programmer.

The third option, I realized, was to create a bigger team to fight Herobrine. The best person we could possibly have on our team would be Steve from Minecraft. I didn't know how to get Steve. Because I didn't know if he was on Earth or where he was.

If he was in the Minecraft game, I didn't know how to get in contact with him. Would I have to enter the game? I didn't know.

6

Henry talked to Anna a little bit about Minecraft. She knew a lot, even though she hadn't played it that much. She mostly lived in the jungles, which was crazy to Henry. He couldn't imagine living without a big soft bed and electricity and instant hot chocolate.

Henry loved hot chocolate.

Anna said she had to go work on something and so now Henry was standing here alone. He saw Stevi was sitting by the pool. He knew she was thinking and it would probably better to leave her alone. She had to figure a way out of this situation. He was glad he wasn't the leader. He didn't have to think about these monumental things.

He saw Edwin sitting in the corner, all alone.

Henry didn't feel bad for him. Edwin was the worst. The first time Minecraft came into real life Henry and Edwin had a battle. Basically, Henry had to get diamonds for Stevi. Henry and Edwin went mining. They were supposed to mine as fast as possible before it was too late for Stevi. It was only them.

Edwin tried to steal the diamonds and hurt Henry. But Henry won the battle. He never told Stevi or anyone else about it. He didn't think it mattered, because ultimately he'd won the battle and had gotten the diamonds to Stevi. Also, Henry was homeschooled and would never have to see Edwin again. Until recently when Stevi invited Edwin on the mission.

Henry probably should have explained why it was a bad idea. It was too late now. And already Edwin was causing problems and being a cry baby.

Henry decided that now would be a good time to deal with Edwin. He walked over to him and sat next to him.

"What do you want?" said Edwin.

"I want you to listen."

"I don't care what you have to say. You're just a dummy," he said.

"If you do anything to endanger this mission, I will hurt you. Understand?"

Edwin went to punch Henry, then stopped right before his fist got to Henry's face.

Henry flinched.

Edwin started laughing. "You flinched. You're just a loser."

"You better not do anything to endanger us," said Henry. "Last time, you almost got Stevi killed. I'm not going to let you this time."

Edwin covered his ears with his hands and said, "LA, LA, LA, LA, LA, LA, NOT LISTENING."

Henry got up and walked away. He'd made his point. Still, he was afraid that Edwin would do something selfish to endanger them all. He'd have to keep his eye on him.

The only other option we had was to give up.

Basically these were the four options:

One—fight Herobrine together.

Two—find a Minecraft programmer who could banish Herobrine from Earth.

Three—create a bigger team. Perhaps Steve and Alex could help.

Four—give up and let the army fight Herobrine.

The first three options seemed impossible to me. I didn't know any Minecraft programmers except Larissa and those white suit guys and they were under Herobrine's spell. I didn't know where to find Minecraft programmers. I didn't think we could beat Herobrine if I was being honest. And I didn't know how to find Steve.

It seemed like our only REAL option was to just give up.

8

I'd taken off my socks and tennis shoes and they were beside me now. I watched my feet dangle in the water. They were extra white because of the glow.

My head was sunken.

The truth was: this whole thing was a failure.

I wasn't paying attention, and Henry unexpectedly showed up beside me and sat down beside me. He took off his shoes and rolled up his pants.

"How is the thinking going?" he asked.

"Bad."

"What's wrong?"

"We can't beat Herobrine, Henry." I admitted. I wouldn't admit this to any of the others. But Henry was okay to tell stuff to.

"What else can we do, though?" he said.

"The only other things we could do would need a Minecraft programmer."

"Notch," he said.

"Notch!" I said it back sarcastically. "The main maker of the game! We don't even know where he lives."

"Yes we do," Henry said. "He lives in Holland."

"How are we supposed to find him, dimwit? Holland is a big country."

Henry rubbed his noise and made a sniffling sound.

I looked at him, because for a moment I thought he was crying. Which would have made me mad, because I didn't like cry babies. He wasn't.

"We can probably find him," Henry said. "He's super rich. He probably has a big house. It would be like finding diamonds in Minecraft. It might take time and might be difficult, but we have to try."

That was true.

"How do we get to Holland?" I asked.

"A flying machine," he said. "We build our own."

"Wouldn't work," said Anna, sitting beside us now. She explained: "Herobrine is controlling the skies. He's even mind-controlled birds to be on the lookout for people. That's why I had to build my base underground."

"Then we go underwater," said Henry. "We build a submarine."

9

Henry was right, though it took me a few seconds to admit it to myself. I did, though. Good leaders are supposed to listen to other people's ideas. That's something my dad always tells me.

I got up out of the pool and yelled to the other boys:

"Time to build. We don't have much time."

And it was true. The more time Herobrine lived in the this world, the more time he had to destroy it. We had to build an entire submarine and then travel all the way to Holland and then find Notch. It was the only option.

"Henry is my co-leader," I announced. "Listen to his instructions."

Edwin spit when he heard me say that. He then crossed his arms.

I ignored him. I didn't have time to argue.

"We don't have much time."

Anna joined in: "Herobrine might find us down here. So we need to build fast."

She might have jinxed us, because right then the ceiling cracked just a little and the Earth shook just a little.

"Do you think that was a natural earthquake?" I asked.

"It was probably him," Anna said.

"Guys, we need to work fast."

Henry and I immediately got to work and began giving instructions. We needed to build a submarine, and then load it onto the mine cart than Anna had in here. She said the track led out to the ocean. To a cliff, actually. We would need to load it up on the mine cart, get inside, and then roll ourselves off the CLIFF! She said there were sharp rocks at the bottom of the cliff, but that we could avoid them if we got enough speed.

First thing, of course, we had to build the submarine.

10

As I mined away, I talked to Henry—getting two things done at once. "We don't need to worry about symmetry and making it look nice," I said—which is something we usually worried about when we played Minecraft together.

We didn't need diamond floors and a gold ceiling. Right now, we had to be practical. The only thing we needed to worry about was speed. We needed to make sure that this submarine went really, really, really fast.

Holland was REALLY far.

I hadn't checked a map yet, but from what I'd heard about Holland, it was pretty far away. That was the other thing. We would need a map.

We figured that once we got in the water and got away from Herobrine, we would stop at a port and find a map —Edwin said that he'd seen maps before in gas stations. How hard would it be to find a gas station in South America? I asked Anna. She said in the cities, they were easy to find. So all we really had to do was find a port near a city. We also needed to make sure we had plenty of food so we didn't starve.

We needed a lot of materials to build the submarine. It would take several hours, so I'll probably just skip the details and, in the next chapter, get to the part where we begin our submarine journey. So read the next chapter, because that's coming next.

11

Our submarine was built, and Herobrine was really close to finding us. The ceiling had cracked even more and even a few small rocks fell out from the ceiling. He was probably bashing the Earth to pieces all around, creating pits, digging, looking for us. The slides had saved our lives and bought us a lot of time because they took us so far underground (if you remember, my slide had a STRAIGHT DOWN drop for, like, a long time).

The outside of our submarine wasn't very nice.

The inside wasn't very nice.

But we did make sure that there was a lot of space inside.

We only had one problem: we didn't have any gasoline. Oh, and we didn't have an ENGINE to go with the gasoline. Basically, our submarine couldn't go.

Henry pointed out that we could put oars on the sides of it and we could all row. Then, when we got to the closest port, we could buy gasoline and an engine from someone with a boat. We could then attach the engine to our submarine.

It was a good idea.

I realized we could mine some gold or diamonds to pay for the gas and the engine. Luckily, Anna had a pool full of diamonds. We broke the diamond blocks up. We didn't have a fortune falling enchantment, so we got six diamonds from the six blocks.

The diamonds were pretty big in real life, so I was sure they would be more than enough to pay for the final materials we needed.

We put the submarine on the mine cart—it was obviously much bigger than the mine cart and we had to balance it. Then we all got inside. We had to make sure we were balanced in the inside so the sub wouldn't fall off the mine cart. If too many of us were on one side, it would fall off the cart.

There were seven of us, so we put three boys on one side. And two boys, Anna and me on the other side since Anna and me were smaller.

We had put a stopper before the mine cart so it wouldn't roll forward until we were ready.

"Ready!?" I yelled.

Everyone shouted back. "Yes!"

Zack 3 farted.

I pulled the lever and the block in front of the mine cart broke, and we started rolling.

If we didn't get to Notch in Holland, the world would basically be destroyed. It was a pretty important mission.

The mine cart—and the submarine—rolled through the cave. It was pitch black dark, and we couldn't see anything. We also started gaining more and more speed because the submarine was heavy.

"Is it supposed to go this fast?" Henry asked Anna.

"No!" she said.

"How much longer until we reach the outside?"

"In a minute."

Once the track went outside and we were in the open, Herobrine would see us right away. So it was a good thing we were going fast. We had to escape from South America FAST.

13

Alex, still stuck in the Minecraft game, was riding a horse and she was going as fast as she could—riding to Steve's house. She'd figured it out. She'd figured out how to get to Earth!

It had taken her a long time of thinking and testing out some different ideas and talking to people, but she'd figured it out!

She needed to find Steve. Even though he was being a downer earlier, she knew he would help go into the world to fight Herobrine.

She arrived at his giant house and pulled up at the front gate. He had a keypad where you had to enter a code. She entered the numbers. The gate slid open.

She rode down his long driveway to his castle home.

She jumped off the horse and knocked on his giant door.

She knocked more. Louder. LOUDER.

Finally, he opened the door.

"I know how to get to Earth," she said. "Are you coming with me?"

"Yes," he said. "We need to leave quickly. I got news that Herobrine kidnapped my friend Stevi."

Alex's eyes widened. "That's terrible."

"Yeah, it is. We need to gather all the supplies we need and leave immediately. We need to bring everything necessary to kill Herobrine."

"That'll take some time," said Alex.

"We have to, though," said Steve.

"Suddenly I'm nervous."

"Me too."

Alex took a breath. "Let's get to work."

14

We'd built the submarine in such a way that we had a big window at the front—so we could see where we were going and see all the cool creatures in the sea.

But we didn't stop there.

We made a line of windows on each side, the left and the right, so that we'd be able to see out from all angles. We put two glass windows in the back.

Right now, in the pitch dark cave, we couldn't see anything.

We could only hear our mine cart's wheels rolling really fast. We could sometimes see flashes of sparks rise up past our side windows. The submarine was really heavy for the small mine cart to carry. The wheels were really loud.

Finally, we broke into the open, into the outside. And we all got blinded for one second from the bright sun. It was a sunny day down here in South America.

I shielded my eyes as they slowly adjusted to the light and heat. Then I could see out the front and side windows—we were in a giant green field. There were trees here and there, but mostly it was an open field. I could see the ocean directly ahead of us—about the length of a few football fields away. We were rolling pretty fast so we'd get there soon.

I hoped.

I looked around, and tried looking up—we'd forgotten to put any glass in the ceiling. That was a mistake. Now we couldn't see if Herobrine was over our heads.

I looked out the side windows, looking up. No signs of Herobrine yet, though I did see some birds. Anna had said the birds were Herobrine's lookouts.

Right about now is when the ground started rumbling.

Herobrine had already found us.

"Great," said Henry.

"We're not going to make it," said Edwin, intently looking ahead at the ocean.

It was pretty far away. Edwin knew from our recent experience that Herobrine could make earthquakes happen pretty fast. If he derailed us, we'd never make it to the ocean.

We'd never escape.

We'd never make it to Notch.

15

"This guy never gives up," said Zack 3, which was the first thing he'd said in awhile.

"We never give up," Zack 1 said.

Zack 2 responded: "I give up all the time."

"Just hold onto your oar and don't move," I said.

We couldn't afford to move out of our places and unbalance the submarine.

The Earth started shaking and, in response, our submarine started slightly shaking up and down. Then more. Then more. And then more.

And then we were shaking side to side.

"Hold on," I shouted once more as everything around us became very loud.

The cliff that led to the ocean was about two hundred yards away at this point. I didn't have much time to take in the scenery around us, though it was very nice: there were very tall trees like I'd never seen before. They were very green and looked to have fruit growing on them. They were swaying side to side majorly—about to be destroyed by Herobrine.

I even saw two monkeys hanging at the top of a tree, looking very scared.

Poor monkeys!

I wanted to tell them sorry, but I realized Herobrine wasn't my fault.

It made me want to stop Herobrine even more seeing the poor, sad and confused monkeys just hanging there in the tree and shouting monkey noises: "HOoo! HoOO! HaA! HAAA!"

The ground cracked slightly in front of us, across the train track!

We rolled over the top of it, and the mine cart and submarine jolted up and down. I knew we were going to get derailed. But we rolled over it and continued. And continued rolling.

We were still going!

"We're not going to make it!" Edwin yelled, sounding very scared.

"HOLD ON!" I yelled.

16

We had one football field left. Well, not a literal football field. But about the length of a football field. I realized two things.

One, we had enough speed to fly off the cliff and make it over the rocks below. Anna had been concerned about that—she didn't need to be anymore. We were going faster than ever.

Kind of scary fast.

I was really afraid we were going to fall off the mine cart. The submarine was too big to push if we fell off. And it would be hard to push over dirt and grass.

That brings me to the second thing I realized—that Herobrine hadn't been directly over us or near behind us until now.

The birds must have signaled to him that we were over here, and he started up the earthquake. But he wasn't near us and therefore the earthquake wasn't that powerful.

But now he was behind us.

I glanced back through the glass and saw him flying

overhead, flying fast, getting even nearer to us. The nearer he was, the more powerful the earthquake became.

He could have destroyed the ground underneath us already, but he was waiting to get closer, so that he could create a more powerful earthquake and destroy even more earth under our feet than normal. He was definitely getting stronger the longer he was on Earth and the more he exercised his power.

"We're going to make it," yelled Anna.

Which gave me a slight bit of hope. But I was confused why she'd yelled it, because the closer Herobrine got the more I knew that we weren't going to make it.

She probably didn't understand Herobrine as well as I did.

We had about half a football field of length left until we got to the edge of the cliff. The ground in front of us split across the track again. We rolled over it with a loud THUD, and the submarine jolted up and down very violently. This time, though, the submarine shifted a bit sideways on the mine cart so it was unbalanced.

The whole thing started leaning to the right, where all the Zacks were.

"Zack 1! Get over here."

He needed to get to the left side, my side, to balance it out before it fell.

On cue, all three Zacks started coming to this side. They all thought they were Zack 1. "No, only one of you," I yelled.

It took them a few moments to decide who would stay and go. I knew for sure we'd fall off the mine cart, but they figured it out in time and the Zack that I referred to as Zack 2 ended up coming to the left side of the sub.

The giant machine we'd built balanced out just in time, but then the Earth started creating rolling waves again. We rolled over one and got some air. We went up about a foot and then crashed back down to the tracks. The submarine leaned to the left and right and forward, every which way, barely keeping its balance.

We each had hold of an oar. The oars, the way we'd built it, went through slime blocks beside us and out into the open. That way we could paddle once we were underwater.

Edwin fell over, losing grip of his oar, and the sub started leaning extra far to the right again. That's when another rolling Earth wave hit us—this time FROM THE SIDE.

17

It hit us from the right side and the submarine flew up off the mine cart and landed back down on it. It began leaning left.

"Zack, get back to your side."

He did and the submarine balanced out.

We only had about twenty-five yards left.

That was seventy-five feet.

We were almost there.

SO CLOSE.

That's also when the Earthquake finally ended—and Herobrine destroyed all the Earth around us and created a giant pit. This is where we would all die.

Herobrine had won.

18

A wave had hit us—a giant wave—just before Herobrine had created the new canyon. The wave caused us to fly up into the air, far off of the mine cart.

We flew into the air for a few good and long seconds before we started to fall. That's when I realized that we had a bit of hope. The water from the ocean was rushing into the newly created canyon, and we were flying towards the water!

We had a chance to make it!

"We're going to make it," said Anna, as if she knew.

She might have been right.

That final wave had hit us so perfectly, and we had been going so fast down the track, that we had a lot of air and were flying pretty fast—FORWARD.

Toward the ocean.

I heard Herobrine growl—it sounded like anger.

Maybe he knew we were going to make it. But I wasn't so sure. It would be close. I could hear the air around us as we fell through it. None of us were holding onto our oars anymore. We were all suspended in the air, watching through our giant front window as we shot like a bullet towards the water.

"What about the rocks?" I yelled to Anna.

"I don't know."

We would have to fly far enough forward to clear the sharp rocks. As we flew through the air, I noticed that the ocean water was rushing into the canyon. If we were lucky, it would fill up deep enough that we could land in the newly formed "lake" and then paddle out into the ocean.

Those were our two possibilities—land in the water that was filling into the canyon and hope it was deep enough for our submarine to safely land. Or fly far enough forward to clear the new canyon and the sharp rocks that were harbored beneath the cliff.

Giant waves of water were crashing into the canyon.

The OCEAN was POWERFUL.

I'd never been on the ocean in a boat. I'd only swam in the ocean a few times when I'd visited the beach with my parents and one time with my friend.

I always liked it—liked to build sand castles and boogie board and whatnot.

Sometimes it was really cold, but unlike my friends, I didn't mind.

And to think: this whole adventure started when I'd jumped into the freezing cold pond water to catch a fish. And now it would likely end in the water. It would certainly end if we all DIED right now. If we crashed down in shallow water and our submarine broke to bits, we might live—but Herobrine would certainly kill us. We escaped him once because Anna saved us at the last moment. She was basically a miracle. But would we get another miracle? That would be two miracles in ONE DAY! We needed another miracle.

I prayed and hoped because I didn't know if we had a chance.

I didn't know if we'd survive this landing.

And from the looks of it, we'd land in about thirty seconds.

19

As it turns out, thirty seconds is a long time. I was biting my nails the whole time. Well, not literally. My stomach felt really tight—because I knew this was the final answer to whether or not we would live or we would die.

As we fell fast toward the ground, it became clear that we would not make it over the sharp rocks at the bottom of the cliff. We wouldn't even make it to them. We were going to land down in the newly formed Herobrine canyon.

A lot of water had gathered at the front of the canyon. We would land in it. The only question was: was it deep enough?

Ten.

Nine.

Eight.

I was counting down in my mind.

Seven.

Six.

Five.

Henry yelled: "I think we're going to make it."

I hoped he was right.

Four.

Three.

Two.

"AHHHHHHHH!" Anna started screaming, followed by everyone else.

I held my breath on instinct.

ONE.

We hit the water and submerged beneath it. We'd fallen from a great height and, like a diver jumping from a tall diving board, we shot into the water.

There was a ton of bubbles in front of all the glass windows, blocking our view. We couldn't see what was happening or if we would hit the stone floor.

Our submarine held together, though.

So far, so good.

We were submerging fast, shooting down into the water.

I looked through the glass window behind us and saw we were creating a sharp trail of bubbles. A slipstream. In other words, we were going fast.

I could tell we were going fast based on the noise of the water all around us, rushing past us. Now I was screaming along with all the others. We were on our bellies now, trying to hold onto the floor of our sub. Since we'd hit the water so hard, we'd all slipped back toward the back end of the sub. But we were still all alive.

Finally the bubbles began clearing away.

We were still going fast.

We could see that the ground floor—made of rocks and broken trees—was looming ahead. We were headed right for it.

"To the oars!" I yelled.

I could tell that there was a chance to survive this.

I got to my feet, but we were at an angle, practically doing a nose dive into this water. Which made me start to slide forward. But I caught hold of my designated oar.

The others were scrambling to get to their positions. The more coordinated ones had already reached their oars—like Anna and Henry and Edwin. The three Zacks were having a tough time.

"Row BACKWARDS!" I yelled.

It was hard to move the oars. I had to pull really hard and use all of my weight because we were going so fast. I rotated it back one time. Then twice.

The floor was twenty feet away.

"Row!" Anna yelled like our lives depended on it, because they did.

Two of the Zacks had made it to their positions. They began pulling at the oars.

We were slowing.

But were we slowing fast enough?

20

"Pull!" Henry yelled, rowing as hard as he could.

"It's working!" I yelled, which was the first positive thing I'd said in awhile. But I believed it. It looked like we were going to make it this time.

I kept rowing, harder and harder.

My head was ALREADY starting to sweat.

I didn't pay any attention.

I simply KEPT ROWING.

Our submarine reached the floor and our front glass window touched the stone with a thud—and for a moment I thought the glass would break. But it didn't. We'd slowed down enough, and now we were stopped. And safe!

We'd made it.

We all began shouting with joy, resting from rowing for only a moment.

"We need to get out of the canyon," I said, beginning to row us backwards, away from the floor. We all started up without talking. We got our submarine off the floor and straightened it out so that we were looking out into the ocean.

Then we started rowing forward as fast as we could. I was afraid Herobrine would cause another earthquake while we were still in this canyon. We needed to get out into the open ocean.

We rowed as hard as we could, knowing what it meant.

We got a pretty good speed going since there were many of us.

We reached the end of the newly formed canyon where the canyon and ocean met. We saw the tall sharp rocks that went all the way up to the surface—the ones Anna had been scared we'd land on.

We turned to the right simply by one side rowing less than the other, and veered around them. Then we were in the open ocean.

The only problem I knew of was that Herobrine knew we were here and was most certainly watching us. Would he continue trying to attack us? Earthquakes wouldn't affect us now that we were underwater. We were safe from earthquake attacks. But Herobrine had a lot of different kinds of attacks he could launch.

Now that we were out of the canyon and in the REAL ocean, I saw that the water was much more blue and it was much deeper out here. Like, hundreds of yards deeper. We couldn't even see the ground floor.

"Submerge!" I yelled.

And Henry took the wheel that we'd placed at the front of the submarine. The wheel was made of sticks and spider webs. We bent the sticks into a circle and tied them together with webbing. It was a pretty good invention.

He aimed us downwards.

I wanted to go deeper underwater so Herobrine

wouldn't be able to see us as well.

"He can mind control fish and squids," said Anna.

And just then a squid swam in front of us.

It made us all scream, but then I remembered that squids were harmless. This one wasn't being mind controlled because it just kept swimming, out of our way.

We submerged deeper and deeper into the ocean, and I felt like we were safe.

Until we heard the giant GONG noise, like a giant cymbal ringing out under the water. Henry and I immediately knew what it was. Anna knew a lot about Minecraft, but she didn't understand what this meant.

"What?" she asked.

Right about then, we saw it. It was directly blocking our path. It was an UNDERWATER TEMPLE. We heard the GUARDIAN speak in a different language. It sounded super scary.

"Sounds scary!" yelled one of the Zacks.

Guardian's were scary. Very scary.

If Herobrine started to mind control the guardian, then we were as good as dead.

"We need to go around it," yelled Henry.

That was a good idea.

We changed our rowing so that we would go around the temple. The guardian wouldn't come out and attack us, right?

But then something weird happened that never happened in the Minecraft game—so I knew it was Herobrine's doing. Some kind of underwater whirlpool developed, and we started getting sucked towards the underwater temple.

"What's happening?" asked Edwin.

"Herobrine is controlling the water! Or the temple or something. We're getting sucked towards it."

"Paddle harder," I said.

But it was no use.

We tried and we tried, but the whirlpool only got more powerful.

We eventually gave up and watched as we were sucked towards the underwater temple—toward a giant entrance in the side of the temple. Herobrine would suck us into it, and the guardian would kill us. This is probably the end, dear readers.

I'm pretty sure that this is how the story ends.

Episode 4

1

Welcome, one and all, Minecraft lovers, players, and people. This is episode 4 of "Herobrine In Real Life" and in case you forgot what happened in the other books or you haven't read them yet, I'll fill you in really quickly.

Basically my friends and I were kidnapped by people in white suits who told us they were Minecraft game makers and that they needed our help to defeat the evil Herobrine who had come into real life—our world, planet Earth. He got out of the game somehow and was now in our world, trying to destroy it.

As it turned out, Herobrine was mind controlling the white suit people. It was really just a trap by Herobrine to try to kill me and my friends. I still haven't figured out why he was trying to kill me though. It didn't make any sense.

Anyway, the white suit people dropped us off in a canyon—a giant pit—created by Herobrine to try to kill us. We barely escaped and went on the run. We almost died at one point, but we were saved by a girl named Anna, who is a local girl who lives in one of the villages down here in South America. She joined our team to try and stop Herobrine.

We realized there was only one thing we could do to try and stop Herobrine—we had to build a submarine and travel underwater, through the oceans, to get to Notch. Notch is the maker of the Minecraft game, the original one. We don't really know exactly where he lives. Somewhere in Holland. It'll be like going on a diamond hunt.

Anyway, we built the submarine, but before we got anywhere, we got attacked by Herobrine. We barely got away, and we thought we were safe for a few moments, until Herobrine started mind-controlling a guardian in an underwater temple!

A whirlpool was created—by Herobrine himself—and our submarine started to get sucked toward the temple. The whirlpool was sucking us toward an entrance in the side of the temple. We tried to get out of the whirlpool, but it wasn't possible.

And that's where this story continues.

Hope you enjoy.

And, remember, this book might be somewhat scary since it's about Herobrine.

BEWARE. Continue if you dare.

2

We'd all given up rowing because it was useless. The whirlpool was much too powerful. There was no way we'd escape it.

Herobrine was using his powers to pull us into the temple. There was a big entrance on the side of the temple, and we were getting sucked right towards it.

RIGHT TOWARDS IT.

I pictured the guardian that I knew was inside. I knew there was a guardian inside because a freakin' gong sounded off as we neared the temple.

I pictured the guardian waiting there to crush and devour us.

We were only one hundred feet from the temple.

This was not good.

"What do we do?" Henry asked.

I didn't have any good ideas.

3

Well, I did have one thought about how we could get out of this. But it was crazy. And it probably wouldn't work.

No, no, no.

I needed to think of something else.

I looked to Henry. "Anything we could do?"

"You already know what we have to do," he said.

He was referring to my idea that I thought wouldn't work. He had the same idea and thought it was a good idea. Somehow he knew what I'd been thinking.

"We have torches," he said. "And we have dynamite."

"We might die."

"What other choice do we have?"

We had no other choice.

He was right.

I tried to think of another option.

Couldn't think of anything.

Guess we had to do it.

4

The idea was kind of like the idea of one person sacrificing themselves for the rest of the group. It was kind of like the story of Jonah and the big fish.

Though it was a little different, because Jonah didn't have to kill the fish, and we would have to kill the fish.

Basically, in the story of Jonah and the big fish, Jonah was told by God to go to a certain city. But he didn't go. He tried to run away. He was on a boat with a crew, and big storms came. Basically, the storms were happening because of Jonah, because he wasn't listening to what God had told him to do.

So Jonah told the rest of the people on the boat to throw him off so that the storms would stop. They didn't want to listen to him at first, but finally they did. They threw him off the boat. The storms stopped.

Then, of course, Jonah was swallowed by a big fish.

This situation was a lot like that. Herobrine hadn't sent those white suit people to get all the Zacks and Edwin. Anna wasn't a part of this until recently. And Henry was just my friend who came along with me. The white suit people were sent for ME: Stevi.

Which is why I had to leave the submarine.

If I got out of it and swam into the guardian temple—then Herobrine would stop sucking the submarine towards it. Because Herobrine didn't care about my friends. He only wanted to kill me.

I had to sacrifice myself for everyone else.

Henry knew it. But he was planning on coming with me, anyway, because he was a good kid and considered me to be his best friend. He didn't tell me he was coming with me, but I knew he was. Because he was Henry.

I went to one of our storage boxes and grabbed a few sticks of dynamite and a stack of torches. I stuffed them all in a backpack and zipped up the backpack.

Henry grabbed a stack of torches to prepare.

"You're not coming with me," I told him. "I know you think you are. But you're not."

"I am," he said. "You can't stop me."

"You better not follow me."

"Too bad," he said.

"Stop being a noob!" I said.

He got in my face. "You're trying to make me sad. It's not going to work. You're my best friend, and I'm always going to fight by your side."

"Maybe I'm not your best friend," I told him. I didn't mean it. But I didn't want him to kill himself with me. He didn't have to. I didn't want him to.

This was all because of me.

I was the one who invited him in the first place.

"It's my responsibility to do this," I said. "And you're not my best friend, Henry. You never were. You're just a dumb thumb-sucking noob. A loser who is afraid of everything and gets panic attacks because he's super lame."

Henry packed his torches and some sticks of dynamite in a backpack and zipped it up. "I am your best friend, Stevi. And calling me names won't work. You've called me names before, and it's hurt. But you also taught me not to let others control my feelings. You taught me to not be a cry baby. I know you're just calling me names to stop me from helping you. But I'm going to help you."

None of the other kids could hear us talking.

Except apparently Anna, because she stepped beside us and joined our conversation.

"What are you guys doing?"

"Stevi and I are going to save you guys," Henry said.

I realized that Henry was different from the Henry I'd first met a long time ago. He was older and tougher now. He wasn't going to take NO for an answer.

"We're going to exit the submarine," I explained to Anna. "Once we exit it, most likely Herobrine will stop sucking the whole submarine into the temple. When that happens, you and the boys need to row as hard as you can and GET OUT OF HERE. Follow the plan. Go to Holland. Got it?"

"I want to help you guys."

I shook my head *NO*.

"We're most likely going to die," said Henry.

She nodded. "In that case, I'll stay with the sub."

Then Anna kissed Henry on the cheek.

His face turned bright red.

"You are cute when you're red," she said.

And he turned even more red.

"Ready, Henry?" I said.
He nodded.

5

We had created a hatch in the floor of the submarine. It was a good way to get in and out of the sub even when underwater, since water won't rise through it.

We opened the hatch and suddenly we could hear the ocean very loudly. I realized that we were about to jump underwater—in the freakin' ocean.

I was really scared of going into a real life underwater temple. But now I realized I was also scared to simply enter the ocean. I'd never swam this deep under the ocean.

What if we got eaten by sharks before we even got to the temple?

I told Anna to explain the situation to the boys. They were oblivious to us right now. Not really paying attention. Then Henry and I looked at each other one more time.

"Thanks, Henry," I said.

He nodded.

I jumped through the hatch and fell out the bottom of the submarine, into the OCEAN.

6

Here's something you should know about the ocean—
it's freezing cold! Henry jumped out right after me and
now we were floating underwater.

Before I took in the scenery, I started swimming
towards the underwater temple. I had my eyes open
underwater, which didn't hurt even though it was salt
water. I always opened my eyes underwater. Plus, we had
no other choice since we didn't have goggles.

It was pretty dark underwater, but there was a light
coming from the temple, which was creating light over the
ocean floor and around us.

I saw a lot of small fish in giant clusters—schools of
fish.

I also saw some really long fish—several feet long. They
were lazily swimming about beneath us. So far, I saw no
sharks.

Since we were in Herobrine's slipstream undercurrent
thing we were being pulled toward the temple really fast,
which meant we didn't have to swim very hard.

Which was good, because swimming hard took up

energy, and energy took up oxygen. We needed to hold our breaths until we got to the temple, which would have places we could breathe. We had torches to set up to create oxygen bubbles.

The temple was a few hundred yards away. It would take anywhere from one and half to two minutes before we'd get there. I was pretty sure I could hold my breath that long, but I hoped we'd get there in time for Henry. We wasn't a perfectly healthy kid—he sometimes had panic attacks and asthma attacks. His lungs might not be as good as mine.

I was swimming in front of him.

I glanced back and saw him, his sheep-y hair waving around underwater as he swam. He looked okay. I kept swimming forward.

I looked up and saw that our plan had worked. Herobrine realized that I'd left the submarine. He wasn't sucking it towards the temple any longer. I glanced back and upwards a little and saw our submarine. The oars were rowing. And they were getting far, far away from us.

IT WORKED!

Henry and I had saved our crew, just like Jonah had saved his.

Then I got sad, realizing what was about to happen. Henry and I—still without any armor—and only dynamite (we hadn't had time to make swords, only shovels and picks and stuff) were about to try to fight a guardian.

I wondered about my room back home. Was I ever going to see it again? I thought about my parents. Normally I didn't get along that good with my mom, but I really wished I could see her again. I thought about my dad. He grounded me a lot. But I was really, really, REALLY sad at the thought of dying right now and never getting to see him again.

I would never be able to play Minecraft again. Or go to school. I mean, I hated school. But still. I would miss some of my teachers, and I'd miss the handball court.

Mostly, though, I couldn't stop picturing my parents in my mind. They would never be able to see me again. They would be really sad.

The thought brought a pain to my heart.

I wondered if Henry was thinking the same things.

Herobrine's underwater current picked up even stronger, and our bodies were pulled even FASTER toward the temple. We were probably going, like, twenty miles per hour! It was crazy. If we weren't swimming towards our death, this would be really cool.

We were closing in on the temple entrance and only about a minute had gone by. We'd reach the entrance in about twenty seconds.

Then we started going fast, and faster.

I was afraid that Herobrine was trying to throw us through the entrance and into a wall—maybe he was trying to break our bones. Because we started going even faster.

I realized that's what he was trying to do.

He was going to try to slam us into the temple wall!

7

The one good thing about Herobrine throwing us so fast into the temple is that the outside guardian creatures couldn't get to us. I also saw a few squids with whites in their eyes—basically, they were under Herobrine's control. They were on their way to attack us, but they were too slow.

I wanted to yell to Henry to swim away from the temple, because we needed to slow down just a little bit. I started swimming, trying to slow. Henry saw me and did the same.

We slowed down a tiny bit.

But then we were inside the temple.

I faced where we were going and could see pretty well since the guardian kept the temple lit with sea lanterns. There wasn't an immediate wall. We flew in-between two giant pillars—and then the current stopped and we were thrown into the center of the temple.

We slowed to a stop, and then swam to the nearest wall.

We needed to breathe.

I struggled to get the backpack unzipped. I got two

torches out, handed one to Henry. We each placed one against the wall.

I took a big breath! The fire was nice and warm. It lasted a few seconds, and I held my breath. Henry's torch was finished, and right then the elder guardian—the keeper of this temple—burst through the floor, breaking the blocks all around, and was swimming towards us!

Elder guardians couldn't break through blocks in Minecraft!

But this wasn't a normal elder. It was an elder controlled by Herobrine.

The blocks broke out towards us.

I had to swim out of the way to dodge one of them. Henry got hit in the chest with a block and it knocked the wind out of him. He would need a torch and FAST—so he can take another breath.

The guardian ROARED.

8

What were we supposed to do?

We didn't have much breath left. We would need to take time to breathe again, but it was difficult to take a torch out of the backpack and post it while getting attacked by an ELDER GUARDIAN!

I was afraid for Henry.

I was afraid for me.

I swam behind the nearest column, and saw Henry swimming for the nearest one to him. I spun around to face the guardian—he shot a beam at me.

The beam hit me right in the stomach and launched be backwards. I flew back through the water about fifty feet and then rammed into a wall. I lost my breath completely.

I took off my backpack to get out a torch.

I couldn't fight the guardian without air in my lungs.

I couldn't fight if I was dead from DROWNING!

As I unzipped the backpack, I saw Henry hiding behind his column. The guardian was swimming about to get a good shot on him. Then the guardian did something strange. It swam toward Henry—more like, darted toward Henry. Henry couldn't get out of the way fast enough. The giant fish creature grabbed him and swam back around the column, holding Henry. Then the guardian flew down through the hole in the floor he'd created, taking Henry with him.

I couldn't see either of them.

I planted a torch against the wall and breathed in and out a few times, then took a giant breath. I pushed off from the wall with my feet and swam towards the hole in the floor. As I neared the hole, I realized that the room down there was really dark—no sea lanterns.

I was swimming as fast as I could, but fifty feet is a pretty long length to swim underwater. My ears were hurting pretty bad from the water pressure—we were deep underwater.

I reached the giant hole and swam through it, down into the dark room. Couldn't see much of anything except vague outlines—corners of walls and the lines of columns. The only light coming into the room was from the hole in the ceiling.

I could tell the room down here was giant.

I couldn't tell where it ended, though.

I stopped swimming and listened for Henry, or for the guardian. I couldn't hear anything. What was happening? Why did the guardian take Henry?

I didn't know why I was asking myself this.

Of course I knew why the guardian had taken Henry —to kill him. The guardian was smart and didn't want to fight us both at the same time. Figured it was easier to kill us one at a time.

The guardian didn't realize that he could easily have killed us at the same time because we had no weapons!

I began scrambling for a torch in my backpack. I got one and lit it. It cast light all around me, and I could see a little deeper into the room. I started swimming deeper in, past giant columns, looking for any sign of Henry. I wanted to scream for him, but I would be wasting my breath.

Instead, I listened.

But I couldn't hear anything.

I put a torch against a column and took another breath. I realized that minutes had passed during all of this. If Henry hadn't taken any breaths, he would have already suffocated by this point.

I wanted to cry, thinking about it.

Instead, I swam deeper into the pitch dark room.

9

I swam all the way to the floor of the giant room and saw that it had been broken—there were a bunch of blocks missing as if the guardian had busted through the floor into the next room beneath this room. I swam to the hole and went through it into the next room.

I was afraid I was going to find a dead Henry.

But instead I found a living Henry, and a dead guardian.

The room was lit up by sea lanterns and I saw that not only Henry was here, but so was Anna and Edwin. They were all floating beside a wall, with torches in the wall, breathing.

I wanted to ask them what happened, but they wouldn't be able to explain since we were underwater. It was obvious that Anna and Edwin had ditched the submarine to come help us. They entered the temple through a different route. I looked around the room and saw a door in one of the walls. It was open. They'd entered there and the guardian must have sensed that they'd entered.

So the guardian decided to swim down to them—but it

took Henry at the same time. Probably to try to kill them all at once. I wasn't sure.

Anyway, it swam down to kill them, but Edwin and Anna were able to kill the guardian and save Henry. AMAZING!

I swam to them and plunked down a torch. Took a big breath. I yelled to them, hoping they'd hear me while I was in my own oxygen bubble. "We need to get to the surface."

"Yes," I heard them shout.

"The door is the exit," Anna said.

I held my breath, and then began swimming for the door. They followed me. We weren't dead after all. My heart beat a little faster from the happiness of being alive. I thought for sure Henry and I were going to be killed by that guardian. Anna and Edwin had saved us. That was the second time Anna had saved us.

I swam through the door, which led to a small room. I saw the final exit door on the right side of this room. I swam to it and exited the temple. It was much brighter outside the door. I plunked down a torch and took my final breath.

The others did the same.

Then I pushed off the temple wall and began swimming for the surface.

That's when I saw a school of squids rushing towards us. They were a few hundred yards away, but they were swimming fast. Much faster than we could swim. They all had white eyes—were being controlled by Herobrine. And they didn't look like they were swimming towards us to have a pleasant conversation and give us high fives.

They looked like they were swimming towards us to kill

us.

I looked back down to the door of the temple. We'd already swam pretty far away from it. We wouldn't make it back inside in time. The squids were fast. When I play Minecraft, squids swim pretty slow. But these were ANGRY squids. MIND CONTROLLED SQUIDS.

I swam faster for the surface of the water.

My friends were just a little bit below me, following my lead.

I didn't know how reaching the surface of the water would help us, because the squids would still be able to attack us. And the land was far away from us. We wouldn't be able to out-swim the squids, not by a long shot.

But as I looked toward the surface, I saw it—two Minecraft-sized boats. They weren't directly above us, but they were coming our direction. It gave me a burst of energy and some hope. I wondered who was in the boats. I had a feeling that the people in the boats would save us.

Of course, I'd been wrong a lot this trip.

It could be more people trying to kill us.

I didn't know.

But we had no choice but to swim to the surface and try to get the people in the boats to help us. The squids were getting closer and closer and I could see that they were two to three times bigger than us. In real life, Minecraft squids can get pretty big.

We were about one hundred feet from the surface of the water, which was pretty far. And it was around this time that I started to lose my breath. I started getting that feeling you get after holding your breath for awhile that you just really want to take a breath.

I swam faster, because if the squids didn't get me, suffocation would get me soon. If we didn't get to the surface fast enough, we'd die from squid or from suffocation.

10

Since I didn't want to die from either, I swam. It looked like I was going to make it. I was only concerned for Henry, who was lagging behind Anna and I.

But then I broke the surface, coming up right beside one of the small boats. A hand was right there, reaching for mine. I took it, unsure of whose it was. I was blinking water out of my eyes as the hand raised me out of the water and, for a moment, I was concerned it was Herobrine and I wanted to let go. Too late. The person dropped me into the boat.

Rubbing the salt water out of my eyes, I saw it was STEVE!

Shocked, I glanced at the next boat over. It was ALEX!

She was taking Henry's hand and raising him into her boat.

Anna had already climbed over the edge into Steve's boat.

It was the legit and real Steve and Alex from the game of Minecraft. They came into our world. And they found us! I'd prayed for a miracle, and here it was.

"How'd you find us?" I asked.

"We heard you were in trouble in South America," Steve said. "We came all the way from the game of Minecraft."

I was breathing heavy, trying to catch my breath, and was cold from just being in the water. Mostly, I didn't notice those things. I was shocked to see Steve and Alex.

I heard a distant ROAR.

I looked around.

Herobrine was far away, high in the sky, flying off the cliff that we'd fallen off of in the submarine. The squids were beneath us. Some of them jumped up in the water around us, but they couldn't get us in the boats apparently. One jumped really close, almost knocking Henry out of his boat with Alex.

"We should get going," Alex said.

I'd never met her before. In my last adventure, I'd met Steve. I couldn't wait to meet Alex, but I couldn't yet, because she started driving her boat away from the dangerous squids, towards the beach. The beach was long and sandy. It looked amazing. Just behind the sand was the large cliff. It was gigantically tall and there was no way we could climb up it.

And Herobrine was coming towards us.

I still couldn't believe Steve and Alex had showed up in the nick of time.

It was truly a miracle.

I was freezing cold now and shivering as Steve drove our boat really fast towards shore. The wind was hitting me and making my nose run.

As we went towards shore, I realized something truly terrible.

I realized that it wasn't a miracle Steve and Alex had showed up and saved us.

It was all apart of the plan.

Herobrine's plan.

Herobrine's very evil plan.

11

Everything made sense to me now.

Before, I'd been so confused. I'd been confused at the white suit people and why they had brought me down to South America to fight Herobrine. I'd figured out that that was because Herobrine was mind-controlling them. Herobrine can mind-control weak-minded people. He couldn't mind-control me or Henry or Anna or Steve or Alex. He could probably control Zack 3, but why would he want to?

Anyway, once I realized that Herobrine had brought me to South America, I was confused. Why would Herobrine want me? He didn't even know me.

Now that Steve and Alex were here, it all made sense.

Do you guys understand what I'm saying?

Herobrine brought me to South America because he wanted Steve and Alex to come try and save me so that he could kill Steve and Alex! I was bait in a trap for Steve and Alex. I was like a small fish that they used on the end of their hook so they could trap bigger fish. Namely, Steve and Alex.

It made sense why earlier Herobrine hadn't straight-up killed me when he easily could have. He needed to keep me alive to get Steve and Alex to leave Minecraft and come to our world.

Steve said it himself: the whole reason he came was to save me.

"Herobrine's using me to kill you," I yelled over the wind to Steve.

"I know," he said, looking back at me.

"You knew?"

"I figured that was his plan."

"Why did you come, then?" I asked.

"Because you're my friend, Stevi. And you would do the same thing for me."

Herobrine roared in the background, flying faster towards us now, and I was scared for all of us. I was shivering, cold, and scared. I wondered if it were possible for us to beat Herobrine.

I guessed we would find out soon.

Now that I knew the truth, I knew that Herobrine wasn't going to go easy on us any longer. He was going to try his best to kill all of us. And he was the most powerful person in the game of Minecraft.

12

As we continued toward the beach, going super fast in the boats, Steve reached into his inventory and produced a set of diamond armor for me. It was made just for me, so it wasn't too big or heavy. The pants were too big for me though, so I just wore my jeans instead. I put on the diamond shirt. I tried the feetings, but they made my feet too heavy and I needed to be able to run fast at all times.

"What else do you have?" I asked Steve.

"Everything, practically," he said. "Everything we could think of. We stashed the rest of our stuff in a box in the cave systems up ahead."

Steve pointed to the entrance of a cave.

I could see it from here since we were almost at the beach.

We were going over the big waves that rolled and crashed into the beach. We skipped over the top of one, catching a couple feet of air. The sun was getting hotter now, which was nice.

Just then, Herobrine, using his powers, broke off a giant chunk of the nearby cliff. He sent the giant pieces of cliff flying down towards us, then he ignited them on fire, which isn't something he'd done earlier. Which meant I was right. He was holding back before.

He wasn't now.

He was sending a meteor shower at us.

I saw Alex looking up.

Then, without slowing down, our boats crashed on the beach, breaking to pieces, and we flew onto the beach. "To the cave!" Alex yelled.

Looking up, I saw the meteor shower flying towards us.

I followed Alex, and we ran into the cave just as the meteors hit the sandy beach. The cave entrance was dark. We turned a corner and there was a corridor filled with torches. It was nice and bright. Alex was running fast, just the way I liked it.

We ran down the corridor—Henry, Anna, Steve, Alex, and I.

That was when everything around us started shaking.

Herobrine was going to break this entire mountain onto our heads.

"Don't worry," Alex yelled as she ran. "Just keep running."

I stopped worrying and listened to Alex. She knew what she was doing, for sure. After all, she was from Minecraft, and was one of the best players ever.

Everything was shaking all around us now, and some of the torches went out, smoke rising up from them, filling the small space.

Then were were out of the corridor in a big open area of the cave. There were torches everywhere and there were rocks glowing in the walls. I saw a pile of mine carts in one corner. Overhead, I saw platforms built of wood and rickety looking metal chandeliers.

We were in a mine shaft!

I loved mine shafts.

Since there were torches everywhere, it was a lot warmer in here.

Still, everything was shaking, and I was concerned Alex hadn't thought this all through. I should have believed in her more, though. Because a few seconds later I saw several mine carts sitting on train tracks.

"Get in!" she yelled.

I loved riding in mine carts!

We needed to get in fast. The rocks were beginning to crumble over our heads. Small pieces of rocks were falling now.

"Run, Henry!" I yelled.

He was just behind me, trying to keep up.

"I'm coming, Stevi," he yelled back.

Everything felt slow motion to me. I couldn't wait to get into the mine carts. I wondered where the track lead to, but I was sure it would help us get away from Herobrine and collect resources. Steve said they had a box full of resources. I wondered if the box was singular or two boxes put together. I hoped it was two boxes put together. We needed all the resources we could get.

Then I was climbing into a mine cart.

Henry jumped in face first behind me, spilling into the cart like the sheep-y character he was. I leaned forward and the mine cart automatically started going. Steve and Edwin got into a mine cart. Anna and Alex got into a mine cart. Then we were going down the track as gigantic rocks fell from the ceiling behind us. A giant rock fell just behind Henry and I, obliterating the track into pieces. It could have crushed us. But we were gaining speed.

I was leaning as far forward as I could.

There were three mine carts and three tracks.

We were traveling side-by-side with our friends.

Then, as this cavern started to completely crumble, we entered a new cavern. This one was darker. Mustier. There were fewer torches on the walls. I only saw four or five, but they were far away because the cavern was huge —they almost seemed like stars in the sky.

The track got steeper.

And then steeper.

And then STEEPER.

Suddenly, we were going nearly straight down into darkness. Wind was rushing against my face. Henry was standing beside me now, because mine carts are pretty big in real life. We were holding onto the front edge of the cart, staring into blackness.

WHOOOOOOOOOOOOOOSH!

We were going so fast!

And I couldn't hear Herobrine at all.

We were escaping.

That is, I thought we were escaping.

BUT THEN I HEARD THE LOUD AND UNMISTAKABLE GROWL OF HEROBRINE. I spun around and I saw the exit of that first cavern. Herobrine was hovering in the center of it. His eyes were bright white, like two flashlight beams practically. He roared once more, then he started flying towards us, FASTER than we were going. And we were going fast! Probably sixty or more miles per hour.

Our track got steeper, which helped us to go faster, but Herobrine was still flying fast.

"He's behind us," I yelled.

Steve turned back and saw him. "If he gets too close," Steve yelled, "and if you look at him, he can teleport you up to him. Don't look at him."

I almost totally forgot that he had that power. We couldn't let him get close. I nudged Henry just to make sure Henry understood the gravity of this situation. "Don't look at him EVER, Henry," I said.

"I know, Stevi," he said, rubbing his forearm across his nose.

His hair was blowing like crazy.

I couldn't barely see him, though, because it was so dark in here.

Herobrine roared again.

I grabbed Henry's hand.

"Are you scared, Stevi?" he said.

He didn't sound concerned before.

He did now.

Henry was used to me being fearless. When he saw me afraid, it made him afraid. I was having a hard time hiding my fear—because, like I said, Herobrine is the only person who scares me.

And right now, I was afraid.

I was terrified.

And I could barely hide it.

So I didn't answer Henry.

I turned around, though, to glance at Herobrine. I looked at him quickly, then looked away so that I wouldn't get teleported. He was halfway closer to us than he had been. His eyes were shining brighter than ever. Then I heard his voice in my mind.

He said, "Be afraid, Stevi."

At first, I thought I was using my imagination, but then Herobrine told me something else: "I'm going to kill you and all your friends," he said to my thoughts.

I knew that it was Herobrine.

Somehow I knew.

I didn't know how he did it, but obviously when Minecraft comes into real life, everything changes—and things that were normally impossible become possible.

"Don't talk to me," I told Herobrine in my mind.

Herobrine laughed out loud behind us, and it was the scariest laugh I'd ever heard in my life.

Next thing I knew, our train track took us into a sharp turn. We leaned to one side of the mine cart, and then we entered through a small opening into a new cavern. This one was bright and long. There were giant torches and chandeliers everywhere. This was a part of the mine shaft that the miners spent a lot of time working in.

The track was straight for a good distance.

We raced into the room, still side-by-side.

Steve and Edwin's cart was beating us by a few feet.

I leaned more forward, trying to get more speed.

There were platforms, scaffolding, and ledges on either side of the tracks. And that's when I saw them—rather, that's when I heard them.

An arrow whizzed by over my head. I looked over and saw a skeleton.

"Skelleys," I yelled.

They were all appearing now, as if out of nowhere. They were standing up on the platforms all around us, beginning to launch down arrows.

Henry and I only had diamond shirts.

We would die if we got shot in the heads!

Then twenty skelleys appeared out of thin air on the train tracks just twenty-five feet ahead of us. They started shooting arrows. All of the skelleys eyes were glowing white, like Herobrine's, which is when I remembered that Herobrine could summon mobs. He could summon any types of mobs he wanted, and he controlled them. He turned evil mobs even more evil, and he could turn good mobs—like pigs or villagers—evil. You can tell if a mob is being mind controlled by if they have white eyes.

AND IF THEY FREAKIN' APPEAR OUT OF THIN AIR!

Henry and I squatted down in our mine cart, putting our hands over our heads.

Arrows thudded into the sides and front of our cart.

THUD! THUD!

And soared over our heads, just missing.

I wondered how we were going to survive.

13

The arrows weren't slowing down our mine carts. We were traveling just as fast towards the new spawns on the track in front of us. I didn't dare move as the tips of arrows pierced the sides of our mine cart.

Then our mine cart crashed into the skelleys. The mine cart jolted around as we plowed through them. I heard their bones. We shattered them! We barely slowed down, continuing down the tracks. Then we passed under an overhang into another area of the mine shaft.

Arrows were no longer being shot at us.

Still, I took a few moments to carefully stand.

I saw that this area of the mine shaft was darker than the last. The light was coming from far below where there were giant pools of lava, hundreds of feet beneath us. There were train tracks everywhere, criss-crossing, interlinking.

We'd entered a giant part of the underground.

Our train track was raised up on really tall stilts.

We were high over the lava, with no floor beneath us. If we fell off the track, we'd fall to the lava. And now we were going down again, picking up speed.

Then our track started going up.

Then it dipped down.

Then it turned sideways.

It was like a roller coaster at Disneyland.

It smelled different in here, like lava.

When you play Minecraft, you don't get to actually smell the lava. In real life, you do. It doesn't smell that good. But anything was better than Herobrine.

Looking backwards, I didn't see him.

Maybe he thought the skelleys would have gotten the best of us. Maybe he thought we'd be dead by now.

Deep down, I knew this wasn't true.

Herobrine was only just beginning to destroy us.

14

As we barreled down the track which was essentially a roller coaster at this point, I yelled to Steve. He was on a different track, and his track winded beneath ours, then he came up on the other side of us. Alex and Anna were on a track that took them high up in the air, but I could see that they would come back down soon.

"Where are we going?" I yelled.

"We're going to where we stashed the supplies," said Steve. "A safe room."

"What's that?"

"You'll see."

"Will we make it?" I asked.

It was right then that Herobrine finally entered this part of the underground. He announced his entrance with a roar. That fear came back to my heart. I was afraid we wouldn't make it to the "safe room."

"This track will take us there," said Steve. "We'll make it."

"But what if—"

I was going to say: "What if spawns appear?"

I was cut off.

Because spawns appeared.

This time Herobrine summoned zombies. They appeared in mid-air, all around the tall ceiling of this giant area. Then he let them fall down towards the track. There were hundreds of them, and I was unsure how we were going to get past them.

"Here," yelled Steve, as his track came uncomfortably close to ours.

But it worked out, because I was close enough that he could hand me a diamond sword.

He handed a diamond sword to Henry as well.

They were perfect sizes for us: not too light, not too heavy.

I swung mine around a little to get used to it.

"Do you have any golden apples?" I asked.

"In the box," he said. "We have everything we need to defeat Hero. We just need the box."

I was confused why Steve called Herobrine "HERO." I didn't have time to question it, though. Our track veered away from Steve's. The zombies were falling towards the track.

Then two zombies landed on the track twenty feet ahead of us.

They landed hard and broke through the track, then fell towards the lava. Some zombies fell onto the track behind them and the track didn't break.

I hoped our cart was going fast enough to jump over the gap in the now-broken track. I didn't have any way to slow us down.

I glanced over and saw Steve was far away from us, fighting zombies that had landed on the track in front of him. He plowed through his zombies.

"Fingers crossed," I yelled.

Then we hit the gap in the track. It was wider than I had originally thought. Our mine cart flew off the last bit of track and launched over the gap. Problem was, the track rose a little. The front of our cart hit the broken track and began to fall!

We didn't make it.

Thinking fast, I threw my diamond sword onto the track as we began to fall. Then I grabbed Henry's hand with my right hand and I grabbed the edge of the train track with my left. Our mine cart fell right out from under our feet, falling for the lava below.

And now we were hanging on from the broken train track.

Henry was really heavy in my hand.

The zombies on the track were making groaning noises, walking towards us with the whites in their eyes. With all of my might, I lifted Henry, trying to lift him up to the track. I wasn't strong enough. I only lifted him a few inches, then I had to let my arm go straight.

My grip on his hand as well as on the track was fading fast.

I looked down at Henry. He was holding onto his diamond sword with his free hand. "Hold on tight, Henry," I yelled, looking beyond him at the lava below. Our mine cart splashed into it, and I heard a sizzling noise as the lava began to melt the strong metal.

"Are we going to die?" asked Henry, looking sheep-ish.

I looked away from him, looking at my hand that was holding onto the track. The big green zombies were only a few feet away. The zombie leading the way had a stone sword, and I knew he would slice my hand off and cause Henry and I both to fall into the lava.

Herobrine ROARED, which filled the entire cavern.

My grip was slipping on Henry's hand.

What to do, what to do? I asked myself as my hands and forehead became really sweaty. I couldn't see Steve or Alex anywhere. Their mine carts had continued going down the track—they'd successfully plowed through the zombies and continued forward.

It was only Henry and I, the zombies, and Herobrine left.

15

"Throw me," yelled Henry up to me.

"No!" I yelled back.

I wasn't going to drop Henry into the lava.

Was he crazy?!

"Throw me, Stevi," he said. "LOOK!"

The zombies were only a few feet away from me.

I looked to where Henry was pointing with his sword.

Beneath the train track, ten feet beneath us and a few feet over, was a ledge of some sort, built between the stilts that supported the track. It was a small platform, and if I didn't throw Henry far enough, he would surely fall into the lava.

Henry chucked his sword toward the platform. It landed, nearly bounced off, and rested on the edge of the wooden platform.

Herobrine roared again as I began to swing Henry, preparing to throw him down. I knew I had good aim, and I knew this was our only choice.

This was exactly why I hadn't wanted to bring Henry on this trip in the first place. I hated putting Henry in danger. He was my best friend in all of the world and, even though he was a nerd, he was the coolest person I knew, because he was a good friend, and he was smart.

I was swinging him pretty good now.

Herobrine was floating near us, and I thought for sure he was going to kill us.

There was a zombie a foot away from me, but the zombie didn't have a sword. He was trying to squat and hit me with his hands but he couldn't reach.

That was good.

Then Herobrine was over our heads, floating past us, continuing to the other end of the cave. He didn't care about us! He only cared about Steve and Alex.

That was good for us at the moment.

I saw Henry's hair waving around as I swung him.

My hands were really sweaty.

For one, it took a lot of energy to hang onto something. It took extra energy to hold onto someone while hanging. You should try it sometime.

For two, it was really hot in here from the floor of lava, which was bubbling up in all different places.

At last though, I realized Henry and I were swinging enough. We swung backwards, away from the platform. Then the return swing began. When he was in the right spot, I let go of his hand and he began falling for the platform. I started swinging away, reaching up with my NOW free hand to hold onto the track with two hands. Henry's feet landed on the VERY edge of the wood platform. He swung his arms in small circles trying to keep his balance, to keep from falling.

He leaned forward and fell to his hands and knees on the platform.

SAFE!

Now, there was just me. My diamond sword was under the feet of all the zombies on the track. I didn't have room to climb up because they were all blocking me.

I realized I had to jump to the platform as well.

"I have to jump, Henry! Move aside."

Henry turned around, picking up his sword, moving to one side of the small platform. I was still swinging but I started swinging a little more so I could reach the platform. It would be a farther fall for me than it was for Henry because I was higher up. I felt like a gymnast, or a circus performer.

Then I finally let go of the track.

My hands felt much better.

I was flying through the air.

Henry was right there, watching.

"You're not going to make it," I heard him yelling.

The warm wind was blowing through my hair which was sticky with sweat.

Then my tip-toes landed on the platform and I slipped and fell. I grabbed onto the edge of it with my hands as I fell, but my hands were so sweaty and tired that I began to fall.

At the last moment, when I thought for sure I was going to die, Henry grabbed my hands. He'd let himself fall down flat on the platform, so his weight was holding me up.

I took a deep breath, then grabbed onto the edge of the platform, started pulling myself up. My arms were dead tired, but Henry helped me. Unlike some little kids, I'd already learned how to pull myself up. I kicked my foot over and rolled onto the platform.

Then Henry and I were laying there on our backs, staring up at the track over our head. The zombies were looking down at us, confused how to get down here.

I could see my diamond sword, sparkling up there.

I really wished I had it with me.

At least I had this diamond t-shirt.

"That was crazy," said Henry.

Herobrine was long gone, out of this cave.

I was too tired to get up.

"Yeah. It was crazy."

I didn't know what to do.

I felt stranded, being right here.

I didn't want to move because I was too tired.

I moved my sticky hair out of my face.

"I'm sorry, Henry."

"For what?"

"For not always being nice."

"Oh, that's okay."

"No. It isn't," I said. "In case we die, I wanted to say sorry. And I wanted to say you're the best friend a person could ever have, and the nicest. And I love you, Henry. Like a little brother, of course."

"Of course, of course," he said. "But I already knew all of that Stevi. I know you don't always say your feelings with words, but that's okay, because I know that you have the capacity to care for people more than most people, and I know you see the best in me when other people don't."

Henry understood me.

I liked having a best friend like Henry.

"And you're the best leader I know," Henry said. "I would trust you, no matter what."

"Thanks, Henry," I said.

Then I got to my feet. I looked around to try to figure out what to do. We were on this little platform, which was kind of like scaffolding that was probably left over from when people built this underground train track. But there was nowhere for us to really go.

16

But there was.

I realized we could climb the stilts that were holding up the track. They were poles, so we would have to climb them like firemen. We could climb back up to the track. We could get onto the track just behind the zombies, if we climbed fast enough and they moved slowly. Which, Zombies were slow.

I explained the plan to Henry.

It was simple.

Henry climbed up first, without a sword. When he got up there, he got up just behind the zombies. They started groaning and walking after him. He started walking down the track, careful to keep his balance. The zombies followed, and when they did, they stepped off of my diamond sword.

Then I climbed up the stilt and got onto the track.

Picked up my diamond sword.

We had to leave Henry's sword behind because there was no way we could climb up the stilts with it. The zombies didn't notice me because they were all agro'd on

Henry.

It was weird to walk on the track. I had to be careful not to fall through them, which meant I had to take bigger steps. Then I was behind the zombies.

I stabbed the first one through the back.

My diamond sword was OP and the zombie died.

I started swinging my sword at the last of them.

They turned around to me.

I killed them easily, hitting some off the track.

It made my forehead more sweaty, but it was really cool.

Finally, they were all dead, and it was only Henry and I in this big cavern. We fist-bumped.

"That was so cool, Stevi!"

It truly was.

We started running down the track, as fast as we could, which wasn't very fast because it was awkward to walk across train tracks suspended very high up in the air.

I could hear Herobrine roaring from the next cavern over. The roars sounded far away and muted. I wanted to get over there really badly to help.

17

I was running as fast as I could, trying my best not to fall between the train tracks, which would mean certain death. Henry had a harder time keeping up, per usual.

Herobrine was starting to shake the atoms and molecules of that next cavern over, where my friends were. It was causing the cavern out here to shake slightly. Then, through the opening to the next cavern, I could see flames. Herobrine was summoning fire.

He could rain down meteor showers.

Now that he got what he wanted: namely, Steve and Alex—he would stop at nothing to destroy them. He would use all of his powers. He would keep creating and controlling mobs. It wouldn't stop until either he killed us or we killed him.

This is why I was so afraid of Herobrine.

There were so many loud noises with the fire and meteors Herobrine was throwing around in there that I was so afraid for all my friends. Even Edwin. I didn't like the guy, but I didn't want him to die. Mostly, though, I was afraid for Steve. He was a good friend of mine.

"We need to go faster," I said, trying to pick up speed.
It was a tricky business.

It took us FIVE LONG MINUTES to reach the cavern.
Going through the opening was shocking.
The cavern was half the size of the giant one we were just in—but this one was completely destroyed. The platforms and walkways that made it a mineshaft were all destroyed to bits and on fire. It was hot and smokey from the meteor showers Herobrine had rained down.
The train track we were running on abruptly ended.
It became a dead end.
I stopped at the very last piece of track and it was a tall drop off. The floor was far, far down there. There were pockets of lava and water at the bottom.
It was really bright in here.
From the fires.
But mostly from the sunlight, which was coming in through a large opening in the ceiling. Herobrine had opened up the ceiling and apparently he'd flown out of this cave, through the ceiling, into the open. I saw gigantic pieces of LAND—the land that was missing from the ceiling—floating up high in the air. He must have been riding on the big pieces of land. And by "big pieces" I mean, like, the size of my entire elementary school. Which is big, because we have, at least, twenty classrooms and an auditorium and a cafeteria and a library.
Herobrine was somewhere up there.
But where were my friends?
"Down there," Henry shouted, pointing.
Far below us, hundreds of yards, there they were. I

couldn't see all of them, but I could see Alex and Anna and Edwin.

"Do you see, Steve?" I asked.

"No," said Henry.

Henry and I were standing side-by-side at the very end of the track. If we slipped, we would fall and die. There was lots of smoke in the corners of the room. A platform of the mineshaft broke off the wall on the right side and fell down in a mess of fire and smoke ALL the way down. It landed far from our friends. I couldn't see the ground floor very well, because it was blocked off by mineshaft platforms and intersecting train track and whatnot.

I looked upward.

The pieces of land were flying higher and higher, looking smaller and smaller as they continued upwards. I wondered two things:

ONE—why did Herobrine leave the cavern?

TWO—where was Steve, and where were the supplies?

As I thought about it, I realized what was most likely happening. Herobrine most likely grabbed Steve, and now Steve was up there on the floating pieces of land, which is why Herobrine gave up on all of us—he mostly just wanted Steve. Then, after he killed Steve, he would probably come back down to kill Alex.

In Minecraft, when you die, you come back to life.

In real life, you just die.

Which meant, if Herobrine killed Steve right now, Steve would simply die and never come back to life. He would be dead forever.

So what was I supposed to do?

Since the track ended right here, there was nowhere for Henry and I to go. I looked down. The ground was hundreds and hundreds of yards down, and it was made up of spots of lava and one little pond of water. Mostly, though, it was made of jagged rock. It was so far down that it was dark. I could barely see. I could no longer see my friends. They'd moved out of my line of sight. There was too much mineshaft stuff up here on this level.

I examined the stilts that held up the track. It was twenty-five yards behind us, at least, and there wasn't a ladder on them.

Henry and I looked at each other as a breeze blew in from the ceiling. Then, an updraft—which is wind coming from below us—blew past us, blowing Henry's hair everywhere.

The wind was drying the sweat on my forehead.

As we looked at each other, thinking, we both realized at the same time what we had to do. It was the only thing we could do.

We had to get down to the bottom of the cavern—we had to get to our friends, because that was most likely where the box of supplies was that we needed to fight Herobrine.

I had wondered why Alex and Steve didn't simply carry the stuff they needed to kill Herobrine in their inventory, but then I realized it was probably too much for them to have to carry. Or, they were carrying some of the stuff, but not all of it. Or, they were carrying everything they needed, but the box had stuff for the rest of us.

Either way, we needed to get to that supply box.

I couldn't defeat Herobrine with only a diamond sword and iron t-shirt armor. I needed golden apples and enchantments and anything and everything I could possibly get my hands on!

First thing was first, though, we had to get down to our friends.

There was no way we could get up through the ceiling to the pieces of land that were floating in the sunny sky, going up and up still. They were higher than ever, and I hoped Steve was doing okay. I hoped he had enough stuff in his personal inventory to fight Herobrine.

There was no way to get to the sky, but there was a way to get to the cavern below. Henry and I had thought it at the same time. I'd seen it in his eyes.

"We have to jump," he said.

Yes. I nodded.

"I'll go first," I said.

Another updraft whipped our hair around.

Now, we couldn't simply jump off the train track and try to land on the rocks. We were much too high. We would die instantly. We had to jump into the tiny pond of water far below us. If we didn't land perfectly in the water, we would die. The problem was—the pond was far out from us. We would have to back up on the track and get a running start. We couldn't simply jump either. We'd have to dive forward, off the track, to get as much distance as we could. I was ultra afraid for Henry, who wasn't as good a jumper as I.

We had no choice.

I wanted to go first so that Henry could see my technique and speed.

I also wanted to go first because I didn't know if it was even possible to get as much distance as we'd need to reach the pond. I wanted to go first, because if I failed, I would die, but at least Henry would live. I reached out my hand. Henry and I shook hands. Another updraft! Then I pulled back my hair and tightened my pony tail.

It was time to fly.

I gulped.

I walked back on the track until I was a good twenty feet away from the edge. That would give me a good enough running start.

Like I'd already said, it was hard to run on the track. I would need to run as fast as I could. My nerve endings were tingling, and I was feeling lightheaded, which was bad, because that meant I was scared. I couldn't be scared. I needed to know I could do this in my gut instinct.

Gut instinct is this really important thing that works for me quite well, most of the time. If you wanted to do something, especially something hard, you had to have gut instinct.

The problem was the height.

Normally, I'm not scared of heights, but sometimes I am. Have you ever been on a really tall roller-coaster looking down? That's how I felt up here. We were high up, as if we were on a really tall skyscraper. And I was about to dive headfirst off of the track into a tiny pond.

I shook my head side to side forgetting all the scary stuff, ignoring it.

My gut instinct started telling me I could do this.

Henry was standing behind me so there was a clear path in front of me.

And I started running.

I kept my eyes glued to the track, making sure I didn't miss a step and fall off to the left or right or in-between the tracks. I ran faster than I had ever run before. Because I had to.

I was nearing the end of the track, trying not to think too much about my running technique, because I'd learned that overthinking things is what makes you mess up.

I thought about Steve, up there with Herobrine.

I thought about my mom. I normally didn't like her because she didn't understand me or Minecraft, but I missed her right now.

I thought about how this was the craziest thing I'd ever done in my life, and that gave me a little bit of excitement. I like adrenaline.

Then I reached the end of the track. I leapt off of it, from my right foot. I dove headfirst, jumping as far as I could from the track. Suddenly, I was falling in a straight down dive. The wind was rushing past me, and it felt AMAZING!

Imagine going really fast down a roller-coaster, but then take away the roller-coaster. I was practically skydiving.

"Wooooohooooooo!" I screamed, out of mostly excitement.

I had aimed for the pond, and it looked like I was going to just make it.

My hands were out in front of me, like I was a legit diver. I was falling hundreds of yards, really, really, really, really, really fast.

The water was getting larger and larger as I fell.

I saw that I was going to land in the pond.

I could tell.

My gut was telling me.

And then, in a matter of seconds, I SPLASHED into the water.

I slipped through the water like some kind of dolphin.

Since I'd fallen from such a tall place, I went through the water like a rocket for a good amount of time. My hands touched the pond's floor. I used them to push off the floor and I began to swim for the surface. I'd cleared the edge of the pond by five feet, which meant Henry had only a five foot gap to make a mistake. I knew he could make it. I felt it in my gut.

When I came to the surface of the water, I saw Henry splash into the pond, in about the same spot I had. I was taking deep breaths, treading water. I swam for the edge of the pond to climb out.

Henry surfaced nearby.

"That was EPIC!" he yelled.

I agreed.

"We can't celebrate, yet," I said.

"I know," he said.

I climbed up onto a nearby rock, then I reached back and took Henry's hand, helped him onto the rock. We climbed over some rocks and were now standing on a patchy area of land made up of dirt and rocks and pockets of lava. About one football field's distance away, I saw Alex, Anna, and Edwin.

"We're here!" I yelled.

They turned back, waving us over. The three of them were all fighting a giant spider. Minecraft spiders were even bigger in real life than they were in the game. And they were already pretty decently sized in the game. In real life, though, they came in all shapes and sizes. The one that my friends were fighting was at least as big as a Honda Civic.

We ran across the land, towards them.

Neither of us had swords. I'd left mine behind because

I hadn't wanted to jump with it and possibly stab myself.

By the time I reached them, they'd successfully killed the spider.

"Where's Steve?" I asked.

Henry pulled up beside me.

"Herobrine transported him," said Alex, pointing upwards.

So I'd been right.

"Does he stand a chance?" I asked.

Alex was shaking her head, 'No.'

"We need to get to the supply box," said Anna, "but Herobrine keeps dropping more and more mobs at us. We just fought through a mob of creepers."

That made sense. There were craters in the Earth all around from where the creepers had exploded.

"Where's the supply box?" I asked.

Alex and Anna pointed towards a small hill. I didn't know what was on the other side of the hill, but I had a good guess because I saw a giant bunch of light emanating from over the hill. There was a river of lava on the other side.

"We better keep going for it," said Alex, taking a diamond sword out of her inventory and throwing it towards Henry. It landed near his feet. He picked it up.

Then we all started up the hill, even Edwin.

I walked beside Edwin. "How are you doing?" I asked him.

"Not good," he said. His face was extra white and flushed, like he'd seen a ghost.

Creepers were pretty creepy to see in real life.

Basically, all the Minecraft mobs were creepy in real life, even some of the good ones.

Edwin was wearing iron armor—a shirt and pants and a helmet. That was good. He needed more armor than me because he was essentially a Minecraft noob.

When we got to the top of the hill, I saw that a thin wooden bridge was stretched over the top of the wide river of lava. The bridge had no railings. It was a loose kind of bridge—the kind that shakes a lot and swings side to side when one walks over it. It would be dangerous enough to go across if there weren't any mobs. But there were.

There was a giant spider standing in front of it, blocking it. There were three more giant spiders on the bridge. When they saw us rise the hill, they all hissed.

I looked all the way down to the left and right of the river of lava. There were no other places for us to cross. The river was at least a football field across.

The bridge was rickety and scary.

The spiders were practically screaming at us, daring us to try to cross.

"We have to cross the bridge to get to the supply box," said Alex. "We have no choice."

I looked up to the giant hole in the ceiling. It was dark outside. Which didn't make any sense because I was pretty sure it was still only morning.

Alex saw me looking.

"Herobrine turned the sky dark," she explained. "He can block out the sun when he's raining down meteor showers."

"Do you think Steve is still alive?" I asked.

The spiders were freaking out, hissing louder than ever.

Alex nodded. "He's still alive. We'll know when he dies, because when he dies Herobrine will come for us."

"He better live," said Edwin.

I looked at the spiders. They had the white eyes that showed they were under Herobrine's mind-control. Without wasting any more time, I started running towards the bridge, towards the first spider. As I ran, I saw Anna pull out a bow and arrow and begin shooting the first spider. She put an arrow in its head. It hissed, but survived. She continued shooting as I ran towards it, weakening it for me. Henry and Alex were just behind me. Edwin was trailing behind them because he was the most scared.

Believe me, I was scared.

But we had to do this for Steve.

We had to do this to save the freakin' world.

18

Steve had been in high places before, but he'd never been this high. In Minecraft, the sky doesn't go this far up. Earth's atmosphere is taller than Minecraft's atmosphere.

Steve and Herobrine were on a piece of floating Earth, and Herobrine had blocked the sun with really thick rain clouds so that everything was dark. It wasn't raining yet, though.

Herobrine was fully armored up with enchanted diamond armor. He had an enchanted diamond sword. Steve had all these things.

The difference was: Herobrine had crazy powers!

Steve and Herobrine had been sword fighting for the last ten minutes. Steve was getting tired. Herobrine was really good at fighting—he was one of the best sword fighters in Minecraft.

Now the black clouds started to drop rain, and a heavy wind started blowing. It was getting cold up here. Steve's diamond armor was getting cold, but he was sweating a lot so it was okay.

Herobrine swung his sword around, trying to take off Steve's head.

Steve ducked under the sword.

Steve tried to stab Herobrine, but Herobrine jumped into the air and boosted upwards. That was the other advantage Herobrine had. Herobrine could fly!

Steve knew that it was Herobrine's boots that had the flying power. Steve wished vanilla Minecraft allowed a person to make flying boots. Alas, it did not. Therefore, Steve had never flown with flying boots before, only in flying machines.

Herobrine shot up through the clouds and Steve couldn't see him, which was scary. Herobrine would come down any moment, which meant Steve had to spin in circles, watching all around, making sure Herobrine didn't fly in from behind and stab him through the back.

Steve felt bad for all of his friends.

Herobrine had dragged them all into this, using them as bait to get to Steve.

Steve hoped they were doing okay.

19

When I got closer to the spider, it got scarier. It jumped up on its back legs, like it was a horse or something, and hissed. I stabbed my sword right through its stomach. It tried to claw me with one of its hands, but I dodged backwards, taking my sword out of its belly. I backed away as it walked towards me, trying to swipe me. But it was bleeding now.

As I walked backwards and it walked towards me, it died. Then I ran around it, and so did Alex. We were on the rickety old bridge now. There were three spiders left.

Alex went before me, running up to the first of the three spiders.

I heard a hissing noise from behind us.

Turning, I saw two spiders drop in from out of nowhere—Herobrine was summoning more. They landed near Edwin and Anna, and Anna began fighting them.

I needed to focus my attention on this bridge.

Since Alex was running, it was shaking A LOT.

I was holding my sword extended for balance.

Then Alex met the first spider. She swung her sword

around really hard and knocked the spider completely off the bridge. He fell fifty feet down into the hot lava, and I heard his body sizzle when he fell into it. Gross! And yikes! *And ewwww!*

I wanted to throw up.

Spiders were so scary and gross.

There were no railings on this small wooden bridge and I was sweating from the hot lava. Alex was right, though, we needed to get across this bridge.

Get to the supply box.

Save Steve.

Two more spiders in front of us.

Alex ran up to the next one and sliced at it, but the spider dodged back. Then the spider swiped its front leg across Alex, and immediately Alex turned green and started screaming in pain. She'd been poisoned. Alex started running back, towards me, but she collapsed onto the bridge, dropping her sword into the lava. She clung to the bridge as she screamed in pain.

I jumped over her to face the poisonous spider.

I didn't have time to have fear.

Trying to keep my balance on the bridge caused me to run slower than if I weren't on a rickey bridge. The spiders seemed to notice. They started moving a lot to get the bridge to start swinging from side to side. I didn't think spiders were that smart—but then I remembered that Herobrine was mind-controlling them, which meant he was probably watching us right now through their eyes.

The bridge was swinging pretty good now, about ten feet one way and then ten feet back the other way. I was crouched, making my way to the **POISON SPIDER**.

When I got close, it tried to poison me—tried to stab

me with its front foot.

I dodged it, barely.

Then I rolled beneath it and stabbed my sword through its belly since I knew that was an effective way to kill a spider. I pulled my sword out as it fell sideways off the bridge and into the lava.

Sizzle!

The final spider roared louder than ever.

I could hear Alex crying a little bit behind me, but she sounded better than before, which meant the poison was wearing off.

It was me vs. This Final Spider.

It was bigger than all the rest and had a red spot over its heart area, as if it were a giant black widow. I tried not to notice the red spot. I tried not to overthink the situation.

I ran up to it and swung my sword at its right leg.

It dodged back then swiped at me with its left leg.

Its foot sliced across my stomach, across my iron-armor shirt. It didn't pierce or break the armor, but it almost knocked me off the bridge. I was flailing my arms all around, trying not to fall. Then I dropped my sword on the swinging bridge.

The spider swung another leg at me.

I ducked beneath it.

Then the spider jabbed me in the side.

It knocked me off the bridge!

As I was falling, I reached out my arms and caught hold of the side of the bridge. I gripped it as hard as I could, and now I was hanging from the bridge as it swung hard.

The spider tried to crush my right hand, but I let go of

the bridge with my right hand. Now I was only holding on with my left hand! The lava was sizzling beneath it, ready to swallow me up and fry me like a potato. That's when I saw Alex pick up my sword and do a three-sixty jump, swinging the sword around as hard as she could. She plowed the sword into the side of the spider's head and the spider flew off the side of the bridge, towards the lava below.

I pulled myself up onto the bridge.

"You good?" said Alex.

I nodded. "Are you?"

She nodded, then she ran across the final length of the bridge toward the opening into the next cave. I was happy to get off the old bridge. Turning back, I saw our friends on the other side of the bridge, battling a spawn of spiders.

Except for Henry.

He was crossing the bridge towards Alex and I.

Alex gave me back my diamond sword, then she pulled out an iron sword from her inventory.

"The box is in this room," she said as we waited a second for Henry.

"Finally," I said. "Why did you guys put the box here?"

"We couldn't carry everything, and we needed to be lightweight to find you. So we hid the box. Figured we'd come back for it and then fight Herobrine. We didn't realize how powerful Herobrine had become since last time we saw him."

"Makes sense."

"We used to be friends with Hero," said Alex. "That's what he used to be called."

I hadn't known that. "For reals?" I asked. "Like, real

friends?"

"Yes."

"What happened?" I asked.

"He turned evil."

"Will Steve be able to kill him?" I asked. "It might be hard for Steve to kill his old friend."

"That's what I'm afraid of," said Alex.

Henry was here and we started moving towards the cave entrance.

"Afraid of what?" said Henry, joining the conversation.

"Afraid that Steve isn't going to fight his best because he believes Herobrine might turn good. If Steve doesn't fight his best, there is no way he'll be able to beat Herobrine."

We went through the small entrance into a pretty good-sized cave.

It was dark in here, but there was glowing gold in the walls all around. The box was in the center of the room, double-wide, just sitting there. There were no mobs here that I could see. But of course we still had to go down a long stairway to get to the center of the room.

The box was sitting in what was like a circular pit.

We were walking slow and quietly, hoping Herobrine wouldn't summon any more mobs.

It was hard to see the box because of the darkness.

We got to the bottom of the stairway, and the box was only about thirty feet away. And that's when it happened. It was almost pitch black down here. And I heard the unmistakable noise, coming out of one of the shadows, of a witch!

Then I saw it appear from a hole in the wall.

Her eyes were white, and she was holding a potion.

Then I saw five more witches emerge from the darkness all around the pit.

Witches were one of the scariest mobs, other than Herobrine.

This was really, really bad.

20

Steve was waiting for Herobrine to fly back down through the clouds. And then he did. Herobrine came flying down super fast, sword ready to slice Steve it half. Steve jumped as high as he could, jumping over Herobrine's sword.

Then Herobrine landed on the piece of floating land.

"Hero, don't you remember me?" Steve shouted over the noisy wind and the heavy rain. "I'm your friend, Steve."

Herobrine didn't say anything.

He only ran towards Steve, sword ready to fight.

Then they began sword fighting again.

Steve had to duck and dodge and deflect Herobrine's sword. Herobrine was fast, which made it hard for Steve to parry.

"We used to be friends," said Steve.

Herobrine was fighting harder than before and it was causing Steve to have to walk backwards. He kept walking back and back as he dodged and deflected Herobrine's strikes.

Until finally, Steve was almost at the edge of the land.

He ducked under one of Herobrine's rapid swings, and he had an idea. Without hesitation, Steve swung his sword across Herobrine's boots as hard as he possibly could. The boots popped off Herobrine's feet. Herobrine realized what was happening and tried to pick them up. Too late. Steve kicked them backwards, off the piece of land. They fell from the sky.

Steve smiled, because now Herobrine couldn't fly.

Herobrine snarled. "You'll regret that," said Herobrine, trying to stab Steve.

Steve jumped and rolled out of the way, trying to get away from the edge of the land. Herobrine chased him. Steve ran back to the center of their piece of floating land, feeling much safer.

"So you can talk," said Steve. "Do you remember me?"

"Of course I remember you," said Herobrine. "That's why I'm trying to kill you."

"But don't you remember that we used to be friends?"

Herobrine growled, jumping ten feet high and swinging his sword down on Steve. Steve blocked it and stepped back. That's when it happened. Steve had an opening to stab Herobrine in the neck. Steve went for it but, at the last moment, he stopped.

Herobrine realized what had happened.

They were both frozen in place.

"Why did you stop?" asked Herobrine. "You could have killed me."

Steve was slightly shaking, mostly from fear and adrenaline. "I don't want to kill you, Hero. You were one of my best friends. And once a best friend, always a best friend."

Steve threw his sword aside and stood there in front of Hero, unarmed, hoping that Herobrine would remember their friendship.

Instead, Herobrine stabbed Steve right through the center of the stomach. Steve hadn't expected that. Steve fell to his knees, in terrible pain, knowing that he was about to die.

21

Have you ever played *Minecraft Hunger Games* on any of the Minecraft servers? I pretended this was *Minecraft Hunger Games*.

As more and more witches—probably about twenty of them—emerged from the sides of the pit, coming out of the shadows, my eyes were feasted on the supply box in the center of the pit.

In *Minecraft Hunger Games,* the game started like the movie—which I wasn't allowed to watch but I'd watched it anyways. There was a box in the center and, when the game started, everyone had to run to the box and try to get stuff from it as fast as they could. Sometimes people went so fast that you couldn't get anything.

When I'd first started playing *Minecraft Hunger games*, I wasn't any good, and I never got anything from the box. I just had to run around the map trying to find stuff elsewhere.

But then I'd gotten really good at it.

"I'll get the box," I yelled to Henry and Alex as I took off sprinting.

I heard Henry shout. "I'll protect you. Like *Minecraft Hunger Games.*"

I was sure Alex understood to help as well, since she was smart.

Holding my diamond sword in one hand, I ran as fast as I could. I heard the witches making all of those scary noises all around. I was afraid they would start throwing potions at me, but they were still pretty far from me.

I was running so fast, that I wasn't sure if I'd be able to stop very fast in front of the boxes. Instead of stopping, I threw my sword out in front of me so that it landed near the box, then I dropped to my knees and slid over the smooth stone. It hurt my knees, but I barely noticed because I needed to get everything I could out of this box before the witches surrounded me.

I flung open the box.

A witch threw a potion at me and it flew past my head, barely missing.

I knew I only had a few seconds, and I had to make quick work of this inventory.

MEANWHILE, Anna and Edwin were fighting the mob of spiders that were trying to cross the bridge into the inventory room. They were doing a good job.

Edwin was getting the hang of this.

He'd been scared before, but he had pretty decent sword skills.

He saw something falling from through the hole in the ceiling. At first, he thought the falling things were rocks, but then he realized they were boots. They landed in a pool of water not too far away. He wondered what they were. He figured they must have fallen from Herobrine or

Steve.

He wanted to go see what they were, but he was too busy fighting these spiders.

The box had lots of cool stuff.

I grabbed two potions and put them in my back pockets. I grabbed one golden apple and bit it, holding it in my mouth, and I grabbed one diamond sword, throwing my other one aside. The diamond sword was enchanted with knockback. I knew because it was written on the hilt of the sword. I couldn't carry more than that because I didn't have a big inventory like I would have if I were playing the Minecraft game. I could only carry what I could hold.

Now the witches were getting dangerously close.

Alex blocked one that was coming close to me.

Henry started fighting another one.

I got back to my feet and ran back for the stairway.

There was a clear path before me—no witches.

I ran as fast as I could. Henry was behind me now, prepared to fight off any witches coming this way. A potion flew by just in front of me. I slowed down—let it pass—continued running.

I reached the stairs and started up as fast as I could.

A potion landed just behind me and cracked open.

"Go, Stevi, go!" I heard Alex yelling.

Then I was up the stairs and out of the cave entrance.

The rickety old bridge was swinging side to side, but there were no spiders on it because the spiders were all on the other side, fighting Anna and Edwin.

Without slowing down, I ran across the bridge.

22

When I reached the other side, Edwin was pointing and yelling: "Some boots fell into the pond over there."

I still had the golden apple in my mouth, so I mumbled something. I was trying to say: "What does that matter?"

I ran past them, away from the spiders, looking all around the cavern for a stairway or a train track or something. I needed to get out of here, up to the piece of land where Steve and Herobrine were fighting.

That's when I realized: how was I going to get up there? I stared up through the hole in the cavern ceiling. It was so dark outside and the piece of land had floated so far up that I couldn't see it anywhere.

What was I supposed to do?

"What if they're Herobrine's boots?" Anna yelled.

The boots! The boots in the pond!

Perhaps Edwin had been onto something.

With the apple in my mouth, carrying my enchanted sword, I ran for that pond.

"NOT THAT ONE! The other one!" Edwin yelled.

I veered for the 'other one.'

I saw the boots floating near the edge of the water. I picked them up with my free hand. They looked different from any boots that I had ever seen. They had an 'H' on them, which probably stood for 'Herobrine.'

I didn't have time to waste, so I put them on.

Then I stood there, holding my sword, confused.

Nothing was different.

I tried running thinking that maybe they were boots of swiftness.

Nope. They didn't make me faster.

I tried kicking the air, thinking maybe my kicks were extra powerful.

Nothing extraordinary happened.

Then I remembered. *Herobrine had flying boots.*

Taking a deep breath, I was just about to jump when Henry came running towards me.

"Wait, Stevi," he shouted.

I looked to him.

"If you go, Herobrine might kill you."

I was already afraid. I already knew the cost. I'd thought about this, had been thinking about this the last many hours. Henry ran up to me and stopped, breathing heavily from the sprint.

"Stevi, maybe Steve can handle it."

I shook my head, biting of a piece of the golden apple. I put the piece of apple in my pocket and threw the rest away because it wouldn't fit in my pocket. "No. I think he needs my help."

We stood there, in silence but for our breathing and the sounds of the distant spiders. I looked up, through the hole in the ceiling.

"I know you're scared," I said. "I am, too. But we have

to be courageous."

"I'll pray for you," said Henry.

"That's a good idea," I said. Then, without saying another word because we were running out of time, I jumped as high as I could.

Immediately, I shot upwards, toward the ceiling of the cave. Since I'd jumped as hard as I could, I was flying fast, which was scary because I didn't know how to fly in these things and I was aimed for the ceiling! I needed to aim for the hole in the ceiling.

Adjusting my feet a little bit helped me turn.

And within a few seconds, I shot out from the cave, into the open, flying towards the floating land. I was flying, kids! And I couldn't believe it.

23

The air was colder out here and it was raining hard. I thought the rain would ruin my flight pattern, but it didn't really affect it. The wind was the difficult bugger.

It was throwing me around as I tried to aim for the piece of land directly above me. The floating land was very small because it was so high in the sky.

The boots were flying me super fast and I barely knew how to control them. As I got higher and higher in the sky, I started to realize that all I really had to do was adjust my feet and also I could control the boots with my mind.

If I thought that I wanted to go slower, I would start to go slower. If I started to think of going faster, the boots would take me faster.

Herobrine's boots were crazy!

So I told myself in my thoughts to fly as fast as I could. Suddenly, I started going rocket speed toward the land. I veered away from it so I wouldn't crash into it. I started slowing down as I got closer, until finally I was beside it.

I slowed down and hovered—the wind blew me

sideways as I hovered. And I saw Steve and Herobrine. Steve was laying on the floor, and for a moment, I thought he was dead. But then I saw he was breathing.

Herobrine hadn't spotted me yet.

Herobrine was talking to Steve.

"You were never my friend," said Herobrine. "I hate you!"

Herobrine's voice boomed all around, causing me to shiver.

I couldn't believe any of this was happening. The rain was pouring really hard, and I was already drenched. The wind was blowing me around. It was super ultra dark out here. And Herobrine was standing there, holding his sword above Steve's body. It looked like Steve had been stabbed in the stomach and I could see blood, which was interesting because there was no blood in Minecraft. Apparently, Steve had blood in real life.

"Herobrine!" I yelled.

He looked up, shocked. He saw his boots on my feet. Then he started laughing. "You're just a little girl," he said. "Do you honestly think you can kill me?"

He laughed some more, just watching me.

"I was just about to kill Steve," he said. "You want to watch?"

I told myself to fly really fast towards him.

Suddenly I was flying towards him, really fast.

I had my sword ready. When I got close, I swung my sword as hard as I could. Herobrine blocked my sword. With his other hand, he punched me in the stomach and sent me flying in an opposite direction. I was spinning in circles, and I got really dizzy and disoriented. I couldn't tell where I was going.

Next thing I knew, I crash landed on the floor of the land, and my stomach hurt really bad. I looked up, super dizzy, and Herobrine was running towards me.

I told myself to fly!

My body started skidding away from Herobrine, dragging over the land, until finally I flew off the land. Then I put my feet under me and flew upwards, more normal.

Herobrine threw his sword at me.

It sliced through the air, coming directly for me!

I dodged it, flying to the side.

He produced another sword from his inventory, snarling at me.

"Fly back down," he said. "I dare you."

I shook my head 'no.'

He looked over his shoulder, at Steve. Then he looked back at me. "Fine then," he said. Then Herobrine ran for Steve. I was afraid he was going to kill him right then and there. I flew towards Herobrine to stab him the back. I think he'd wanted me to, because he spun around and punched me again—this time in the face. He sent me reeling, flying sideways through the air. I spun back upright.

Herobrine was beside Steve now.

Herobrine grabbed Steve by the hand, picked him up off the floor, and begin spinning him in circles, around and around. Then he let go of Steve, flinging him off the land, flinging him high into the sky.

I started flying towards Steve to catch him, but Herobrine summoned a meteor shower just before me. Gigantic flaming rocks appeared in the air, blocking my flight path. I flew over one, then under one, then went around one. The air was hot from the fire. I wasn't sure how I was going to get past the rocks. Then a rock grazed my head and almost knocked me unconscious. My vision almost went black.

I had to watch over my head to be sure to dodge the additional falling rocks.

How was I going to get through this to save Steve?

I could hear Herobrine laughing behind me.

I couldn't even see Steve, but I knew he was probably halfway to the ground by this point.

A rock about the size of me was in my way. I hit it with my sword. The rock flew away as if it were a baseball and my sword was the bat. Which is when I remembered that my sword had been enchanted with knockback! That meant I could bat away all the rocks.

A rock appeared above my head.

I pointed my sword at it. It bounced off the sword as if it were only a bouncy ball.

Another rock was careening towards me. I swatted it away as if it were a fly.

Now Herobrine was throwing rocks at me.

I hit them this way and that way and every way. He sent one at me from underneath me. I slammed my sword over it and front-flipped out of the way. I was getting pretty good at this.

Two rocks were coming at me really fast, and there was a small gap between the two of them. I dove between them without barely getting scraped.

I heard Herobrine roaring behind me.

He was getting mad. He definitely hadn't expected that I would have a sword with knockback. All of the sudden, with a giant roar, Herobrine summoned the biggest meteors yet and they appeared all around me, coming at me from all sides and angles.

I lost my breath, wondering what to do.

But then I realized what to do.

Controlling the flying boots with my mind, I started spinning in circles really fast. I held out my sword, spinning in circles. I went as fast as I could. The rocks came in at all sides but my sword sliced them in half and knocked them away as I spun in circles.

Then I saw an opening before me and I dove straight through it, telling the boots to fly as fast as they could. I shot out of the meteor shower, trying to get to Steve.

I couldn't see him, but I started a dive towards the Earth far below.

Herobrine summoned rocks in front of me to stop me, but I was getting too good. I dodged them as I flew down and down, zooming in and out of rocks.

Some rocks I couldn't dodge so I batted them away.

Home run! Out of the park!

I could hear a crowd cheering in my head.

Then I saw Steve. He was still a few hundred yards away from the ground. I aimed for him, flying faster than ever. I was slicing through the cold air, through the falling water.

It was super cool.

I was getting enough distance from Herobrine that the meteors were coming in less and less. Finally, I was going faster than the meteors could appear. I was in the open skies now.

Steve wasn't yelling as he fell—probably because he was hurt.

I zoomed for him and, after a few seconds, I caught

him.

I held him in my arms. He was really heavy. Mostly, I just kind of fell with him so that way I didn't have to hold all of his weight. As we got closer to the floor, I started holding his weight. I used all my might to hold him up as we landed, and I set him down on the wet and muddy floor.

I looked up at the floating land.

It was slowly but surely floating back down.

Herobrine couldn't fly, but he could still control the Earth.

"Are you okay?" I asked Steve.

He looked to be in horrible pain and he was holding his stomach. He was covered in blood. "Not really," he said quietly.

I remembered the slice of golden apple in my pocket. I gave it to him.

"No," he said, pushing it away. "You need that to fight Herobrine."

"Eat it," I said.

He accepted it and took a bite.

That would help keep him alive until we could get him back into the Minecraft game.

NOW, it was finally time to kill Herobrine.

I had an idea.

Leaving Steve there, I started running towards the hole in the ground. It wasn't far. When I got to it, I dove straight into it. I was falling pretty fast, and I used the flying boots to land softly back on the cavern floor. My friends were still fighting mobs. I found the golden apple that I'd left on the floor. I swooped it up, then flew back up and out of the cave.

Taking a big bite of the apple, I knew I could do it.
I'd faced Herobrine—my greatest fear.
And I was no longer afraid.

24

I flew towards the piece of flying land as fast as I possibly could. I was getting faster at flying than even in the beginning, and I was really good at it now.

I held my sword out in front of me.

I went as fast as I could straight towards the land and didn't slow down. I stabbed my sword into the bottom of it, which, because my sword was enchanted, split the piece of land in half. I flew up straight through it, then looked down to see Herobrine on one side.

He was looking around, and he saw me.

He laughed. "You still think you can kill me?" he said.

I nodded and took out one of the potions from my back pocket. It said Fire Resistance on it. I drank it. Then I took out the second potion: Swiftness.

Drank it.

Herobrine summoned in a shower of meteors over my head. Instead of flying away from it, I flew straight into it. I batted the rocks towards Herobrine. Two of them nearly hit him. He dodged out of the way. The rocks destroyed the piece of land beneath him, and he began to fall through the sky.

I flew out of the shower of rocks and towards the falling Herobrine.

He was roaring in anger.

I knew that this was my chance. While I had the Swiftness, I knew I could kill him. The first times I'd flown at him, he'd punched me aside. Since I had Swiftness, and since I'd gotten better at flying, I knew I would be able to hit him faster than he could hit me.

Herobrine was intermingled with the broken pieces of Earth and rocks that I'd sent his way. He wouldn't even see me coming.

Holding my breath, I launched towards him.

I shot straight down, towards the rocks.

I held my sword out in front of me. It sliced through the rocks.

I was going so fast through the air that I couldn't even breathe if I had wanted to. It was a good thing I'd held my breath. I broke through some rocks and saw Herobrine about twenty feet out.

He was still roaring and yelling.

I exploded towards him as fast as the Swiftness would let me go.

Before even I realized it had happened, I'd stabbed my diamond sword straight through his chest. I rammed him through some pieces of rock and then continued flying him towards the Earth. I saw Steve laying on the muddy floor, and I flew Herobrine towards that spot.

I flew Herobrine as fast as I could down to the Earth.

And, at last, I dropped him next to Steve.

I landed on my feet in front of them.

Herobrine was dead, not breathing or moving.

The dark rain clouds in the sky started disappearing and all the big pieces of floating Earth landed back on the ground. Chunks of it fell in the hole and down into the cavern. The sun broke through the disappearing clouds and felt nice and warm.

Steve was in pain, but he looked a little better.

To my right about a hundred feet the Earth opened up. Out popped Alex, followed by Henry, Anna, and Edwin. They saw me and ran over.

Alex fell to her knees beside Steve. "Oh my gosh," she said. "Steve. Are you okay?"

He nodded. "I'll live for a few more minutes," he said. "If you can get me back into Minecraft, I'll be okay."

Alex looked to me: "We came through a Nether Portal. I'm gonna need to fly him back to our home." I nodded, and I started taking off the boots.

Suddenly, I was sad.

I had wished to hang out with Steve and Alex more since they were in our world. Once they returned to Minecraft, Minecraft would probably leave real life.

"Good job, Stevi," said Alex, giving me a hug. "It was nice meeting all of you. Sorry I have to leave so soon."

She put on the flying boots, then she scooped up Steve into her arms.

Then she flew away.

We all shouted good-byes.

Then I sat there in the mud, super tired, and sad now.

Within three minutes, Herobrine's dead body disappeared—because Steve and Alex had gone back into the game. That meant Minecraft couldn't be in our world any longer.

Just like that, it was all over.

Anna sat next to me. "You're really brave, Stevi," she said.

"Thanks," I said, but didn't really care.

"What's wrong?"

"I'm gonna miss my friends is all."

Henry sat on the other side of me. "But we're your friends."

Edwin sat in front of me. "And I'm sort of your friend. I mean, we went fishing together."

I laughed. "Yeah, I guess so, Edwin."

I remembered the night that I'd snuck out to go fishing. It was barely any time ago, but it felt like forever ago, didn't it?

It had been a truly crazy adventure.

I'd faced my greatest fear and won.

I, Stevi Karie, had defeated Herobrine.

For some reason, I was super tired and really wanted to sleep.

"Did you take a potion?" said Henry.

"Yeah. Swiftness," I said.

"It must be wearing off, because you look really tired."

That made sense. The potion had given me so much energy, and now I was running low on energy. I laid my head down on Anna's lap and she brushed some hair out of my face, and I fell fast asleep.

WHEN I WOKE UP, we were in a village. At first, I was really confused, but then I remembered that Anna lived out here in a village. I was in a hammock. I got out of it, rubbing my eyes. Looking around, there were huts everywhere and people dressed like Indians.

Anna saw that I was awake and came running over.

I saw Edwin and Henry were taking naps in some hammocks as well.

"Stevi! You're awake! You've been asleep for a long time. I brought you back to my village. I hope you don't mind."

"Of course not."

"My mom found us out there in the field and loaded us up on some horses. You didn't wake up the whole time."

I was still rubbing my eyes. "I guess that Swiftness potion really makes a person tired."

"And fighting Herobrine."

"That's true."

"My mom says she can bring you back to the city today. You'll be able to call your parents so they can come get you."

My parents! I'd almost forgotten about them.

Suddenly, I was afraid.

They were going to be so mad when they found out I was in Brazil. How was I even supposed to explain to them everything that had happened? They would never believe them. They would probably think I was crazy and lock me up in a pound or something.

My face flushed, turned super white.

"Are you okay?" Anna said.

I wasn't.

I realized that my greatest fear in all of the world wasn't actually Herobrine.

It was my mom.

I walked around an hour, pacing about, trying to think what to tell my parents. Anna suggested: "Tell them you went on a field trip."

"To Brazil!" I shouted. "They didn't sign a waiver or a form or anything. And they would ask my teachers and my teachers would deny it."

"Tell them you ran away because you thought they hated you."

"But then they would hate me. Plus, that would be lying."

"Well, you can't really tell them the truth," said Anna. "They would never believe you that Herobrine came into real life."

FINALLY, when I felt like I was going to crack under the pressure, I went to sleeping Henry. I didn't want to wake him up, but I knew he was smart and I needed ideas. So I flipped his hammock upside-down. He fell out screaming like a little girl.

I laughed, which made me feel a little bit better.

He rolled onto his back and squinted up at me. "Why would you do that?"

"Henry, how are we possibly going to explain to our parents why we're here?"

Suddenly his face turned super white. "We're going to be grounded for life."

That's when Anna's mom started yelling something from far away. She was riding into the village on some horses. There was a woman on one of the horses, shouting and yelling, wearing a white suit.

There were a couple of guys in white suits.

The white suit people!

"Where are you taking us?" the white-suited woman was yelling. "What's wrong with you? How did we get here?"

The woman was freaking out and all the men looked

like they were dazed.

Henry, Anna, and I ran over to them as they approached the village.

They weren't under Herobrine's mind-control anymore, and they seemed really confused as to how they got here in Brazil. I could tell because the woman was yelling: "Brazil! How the heck did I get to Brazil? Did you people kidnap me?"

Then she saw me. "I recognize you," she said. "You're Stevi."

The woman hopped off her horse and ran towards me.

For a second, I was scared because she was running really fast, but then she sat down in front of me and buried her face in her hands and started crying.

I got a little embarrassed to see a grown person crying.

"Snap out of it," said Henry, trying to sound encouraging.

"Don't cry," I said.

The woman looked up at me, and suddenly I smiled, because I realized that I didn't have to call my parents. This woman—who was one of the Minecraft game makers—and the men could fly us home. Then our parents would never have to know we'd been to Brazil. We could just say we stayed the night at our friend Edwin's house!

Henry and I looked at each other.

"I'll tell you everything," I told the woman. "But you gotta promise me something."

"What?" she said.

"That you buy us some plane tickets back to America?"

She looked at me funny. "Sure."

All the men came around and I explained to them the

whole story. Their minds were blown, but they believed me. The sheep guy, who had kept making all those sheep noises, was sitting there and listening, completely normal. I didn't tell him about his sheepish antics, because I didn't want to embarrass him.

When I finished the story, the sheep guy let out a big yawn, opening his mouth really wide, and as he did, he accidentally made a sheep noise.

Henry and I burst out laughing.

"What's so funny?" he asked.

I just kept laughing.

That's about when Edwin ran over. "Guys," he said, "I just remembered something. We forgot about Zack 1, 2, and 3."

My mouth dropped open.

Henry and I looked at each other.

The last time I'd seen the Zacks, they were in a submarine on their way to Holland to find Notch.

"Oh my gosh," I said.

And that's where this story ends.

Maybe Minecraft will come back into our world someday.

Maybe not.

Either way, the best thing about Minecraft isn't the fun of playing it: it's the friends that you play it with. And I hope that someday, if you don't have some already, you'll have great friends like Henry and Anna and even Edwin —who was once my enemy but now is my friend.

Sometimes that happens. Sometimes your enemies become your friends, so never hate people, because you might like them later.

In fact, never hate anyone, even if they're mean,

AJ Diaz

because otherwise you might become like Herobrine—a big meanie with no friends.

It's better to be friends with people and even to be nice to people who are mean to you. Because one of the coolest things in life is having good friends.

Until next time, I'll be busy playing Minecraft with my friends, AND fishing. Because I still want to catch that big fish.

So go out and have adventures, and dream big, and have fun, and make friends, and treat others how you would want to be treated. I learned that last part in Sunday school.

And you don't have to be afraid of Herobrine ever again, kids.

Because I, Stevi Karie, defeated him.

EPILOGUE

THE STORY OF THE ZACKS

There is one thing left to explain, and that is the three Zacks and their adventure in the submarine to Holland.

You see, the Zacks didn't get the news that Herobrine was dead, so they continued their journey to Holland, and because none of them are very smart, they had an interesting journey, to say the least.

For the exclusive story of what happened to the three Zacks, visit—

itlpress.com/herobrine

AJ Diaz

MORE BOOKS

Be sure to check the MINECRAFT HIGH SCHOOL series.

This book is called FRIGHT NIGHT. And it takes

place during Halloween. And it's really scary, so get the book, if you dare.

You can purchase it on Amazon or you can get a SIGNED COPY of the book from

<<<<>>>>